AWAKENING INFINITY

AWAKENING INFINITY (Archivist 0)
Copyright © 2021 Meghan Ciana Doidge
Published by Old Man in the CrossWalk
Productions 2021
Salt Spring Island, BC, Canada
www.oldmaninthecrosswalk.com

Library and Archives Canada
Doidge, Meghan Ciana, 1973—
Awakening Infinity/Meghan Ciana Doidge—
PAPERBACK EDITION

Cover design by Damonza.com
Page break by Elizabeth Mackey Designs
Interior Illustration by Nicole Deal

ISBN 978-1-989571-25-5

ARCHIVIST SERIES · BOOK 0

AWAKENING INFINITY

MEGHAN CIANA DOIDGE

Published by Old Man in the CrossWalk Productions
Salt Spring Island, BC, Canada

www.madebymeghan.ca

Awakening Infinity is a prequel novel in the Archivist series, which is set in the same universe as the Dowser, Oracle, Reconstructionist, Amplifier, and Misfits of the Adept Universe series. While it is not necessary to read all the series, **in order to avoid spoilers** the ideal reading order of the Adept Universe is as follows:

More books in the Amplifier, Archivist, and Misfits series to follow.

More information can be found at
www.madebymeghan.ca/novels

For Michael
Always ready for the next adventure. Together.

THE PLAN WAS TO HOP A TRAIN TO OSLO, HANG OUT AT a coffee shop, and connect my personal archive, Infinity, to the Internet. Yes, completely disregarding the well-established fact that magic and technology didn't mix. At all.

I was also hoping to browse as many bookstores as I could before my younger brother's patience ran out. Unfortunately, the five-year-old fledgling dragon was better known for his exuberant—and ultimately destructive—tendencies rather than his attention span.

I almost pulled it all off. Almost proved that my position as Archivist of the Modern World wasn't just an empty title.

Then I got summoned—by the most powerful beings in the magical world. And when the guardian dragons made a request, no one denied them. Not even a lesser dragon.

Not even if it tore me away from everything I'd ever known—and the one person I couldn't leave behind.

CHAPTER ONE

I HAD TRAVELLED TO OTHER CITIES BEFORE, USING THE doorways between the family estate library and other well-established magical archives. London and Paris. Even Athens. But I'd never taken an extended trip by train before—or any other mundane mode of transport, really. Unfortunately, the archival doorways weren't currently an option. I had no ability to trigger them on my own, and neither my mother nor my Great-Great-Uncle Zeke were in residence to open the way for me. So that was how I found myself on a high-speed train barreling its way into Oslo, Norway, with a new tablet in my backpack and foreign currency in my pocket.

Oh, and I had a five-year-old fledgling dragon obsessing over the Norwegian translation for 'hot chocolate and a cookie' along for the ride. And, yes, I'd informed my brother, Sisu, that he was only allowed to order one of each, like a regular person.

One way or another, it was going to be an interesting trip.

My mother, Trissa, had been on a collection with my Great-Uncle Jamal for over eleven months, leaving Zeke to run the archives she oversaw in Giza, Egypt. I knew Zeke would always be interested in scouring any city for unique books with me, but even if he hadn't been busy in Giza, I wouldn't have invited him on this trip. Because he most definitely wouldn't have supported what I was about to try. For a number of different reasons.

My relationship with Zeke was…complicated.

Hence the use of mundane transportation. And the vaguely out-of-the-way destination.

Or at least it was out of the way of anyone who might notice two dragons wandering among the humans. Because dragons weren't supposed to wander through the world. Dragons moved with purpose, protecting the world and all the magic within it.

And I was moving with a purpose. I was just following my own directions.

The trip was only supposed to take seven hours both ways, but getting Sisu out of the house without a backpack overloaded with books and magical objects had been an ordeal, and we'd missed the first two trains. So it was already later than I would have liked. We'd get home way after dark. The family estate was currently anchored walking distance from Indre Arna, a village in the Seven Mountains range near Bergen, as it had been since Sisu's birth. I'd spent the bulk of my twenty-five years living closer to Manchester, England, the estate's traditional anchor point.

But my mother getting involved with a guardian dragon, then having Sisu, changed a lot of things. Children of guardians were rare. As in 'one or two in a generation' rare, hence the need for Sisu to grow up within his father's territories in Northern Europe.

I already had the walking directions to the nearest cafe with Wi-Fi from the train station memorized, and I was about to prove that being the Archivist of the Modern World for the guardian dragons wasn't simply an empty title to occupy me for the next seventy-five years.

Or until I took over one of the major magical archives maintained by the dragons.

All I had to do was to figure out how to link the World Wide Web to Infinity, my personal archive. And even with Sisu in tow, nothing could possibly go wrong in an Internet cafe that I couldn't handle.

Or at least that was what I kept telling myself.

Before embarking on our journey, almost everything I had known about Oslo was at least fifty years out of date. The set of encyclopedias I'd unearthed in my mother's library listed the population of the metro area as 643,000. The main exports were oil and gas, and the average life expectancy was seventy-four.

With my own life span measured in centuries—barring any of the multitude of so-called incidents that had a habit of befalling archivists, whether they were dragonborn or not—being reminded of how short-lived humans were was always a shock.

As we travelled, I'd filled in some of the gaps in my knowledge, collecting real-time information through observation and thoughtful anthropology. That included collecting magazines and maps at each train station, as well as studying human interactions and conversations. As any conscientious archivist would do, whether she was studying the past or the present.

The local currency was the krone, and I had managed to purchase some paper bills and coins from a bookseller in London. He had also supplied the computer tablet currently charging on the seat next to me, though he rarely dealt in anything other than old books, both magical and nonmagical. The sorcerer, Oliver Anderson, had taken over from his father as my mother's primary contact within the world of the Adept—aka those with magic. He hadn't hesitated when I'd contacted him by phone to make my request. My family had established a connection with his own many centuries ago, and Oliver had magically couriered the items to me within a few days via the rune-marked drop point permanently anchored in the entrance of the main house.

Anyone with the proper sequence of runes could send things to the estate. Well, anyone capable of conjuring the magic necessary to do so. As I understood it, it was similar to having a mailing address in the human world. And of course, any unsolicited packages would be immediately confiscated by the brownies who ran the estate. In fact, I was fairly certain they put everything that arrived via magic into an automatic quarantine unless one of the family were around to receive it upon arrival.

Brownies were highly territorial.

Zeke and I had visited Oliver's bookstore—Books, Tomes, and Other Publications—when we'd last been in London. The other Adepts shopping there had presumably taken us for witches or sorcerers, as would any Adepts who might catch sight of Sisu and me today. Even among many of the magically inclined, dragons were still considered creatures of myth and legend, and we were always careful to not shatter that initial perception. I didn't mind playing at a little subterfuge, but doing so bothered Zeke. Because his personal history was also…complicated, and he'd already spent too much time fighting to maintain a sense of self to have fun pretending to be anyone else.

Despite Sisu's urgings to do the complete opposite, I'd been careful to not open the white box that held the tablet—called an iPad—until we'd gotten on the high-speed train and I'd figured out how to attach it to the seat's built-in charging port. The magical energy embedded into every molecule of the family estate might have fried the device had I opened it earlier. Even having it magically couriered while powered down had been a risk. Magic and technology didn't mix well.

But I was hoping the personal archive I was currently gripping in my left hand might prove to be the exception to that fairly hard rule.

Infinity, nicknamed Finny, might simply appear to be a bronze-colored leather-bound book, with worn metal filigree corners, various symbols marking its spine, and deckle-edged pages. But it was actually a magical repository of information, bound solely to me. Yes, I had named my personal archive, though as far as I knew, most archivists didn't.

The aboveground train had been mostly empty until about thirty minutes outside Oslo. And though rolling hills could still be glimpsed from the city, we'd left the Seven Mountains and the family estate far behind us.

As we disembarked at Oslo Central Station, I could smell the ocean but not see it through the eclectic mixture of buildings surrounding us. Keeping a firm hold on Sisu's hand, I allowed us to be swept from the station by a crowd that quickly dispersed in all directions. I had purchased a tourist map, along with a travel guide for Sisu, while we'd waited for the train, quickly memorizing the section of the city that interested me. Specifically the main street, Karl Johans gate, that cut directly through the core of the city from the station to the Royal Palace, passing numerous points of interest along the way.

Still, even as wide-eyed and mute as Sisu had been rendered by the rush of humanity around us, I doubted we'd be able to get as far as the palace without him getting restless. And a restless Sisu—as with any fledgling dragon still learning how their magic worked—would draw far too much attention. Even for Adepts initially assuming we were witches or sorcerers, any outright display of strength or speed from Sisu would cause a stir—and neither of those things were easily contained.

I had fed the city map into Infinity so that I could recall it with just a brush of my fingers against the archive's leather binding. Well, most days at least. Even though my mental link with Infinity was touch activated, our connection was sometimes still capricious. Mom would have said it was a 'work in progress,' and 'as it should be for my age.' I wasn't a fan of either of those two phrases.

But after eleven months without having heard a single word from Mom, I would have been more than happy for her to tell me … anything.

There were a multitude of reasons that a collection could take months, or even years. And I knew Mom was alive because new acquisitions occasionally appeared on her desk in the library. But Sisu and I both missed her. Some days, achingly.

Despite my thick-soled boots, the gray cobblestone sidewalk that edged the pedestrian-only thoroughfare was slightly uneven under my feet. Other than the natural energy sleepily emanating from deep within the Earth itself, the area was devoid of any magical presence—Adepts or otherwise. That strange stillness, even within the bustle of the city, added to my growing sense of disconcertion, of displacement. Not that acknowledging it helped.

Though Oslo was known for its varied architecture, the blocks surrounding us consisted of mostly brick or stone-faced four- and five-storey buildings built in the eighteenth and nineteenth centuries. The street level was filled with shops and restaurants, including some chains I recognized from London. The city was exceedingly pretty, clean and friendly.

Catching sight of my intended destination across the street, I slowed to a stop, stepping back against the nearest building and tucking Sisu beside me to clear the way for the steady stream of pedestrians. I took in the coffee cafe.

Coffee cafe?

That didn't sound right.

Coffee shop?

Fingers flexing in my loose grip, Sisu muttered to himself at the sight of the bookstore on the next corner. I'd noticed it marked on the tourist map, and most definitely planned to visit before we headed home.

Just as soon as I conquered the coffee shop.

Yes. Coffee shop. That was the correct idiom.

Not that I was planning on ordering any coffee. Herbal tea was more my thing, though I didn't drink it often. Something with citrus or honey if I could get it. And a hot chocolate for the five-year-old currently thinking of making a break for the bookstore—Sisu's energy always shifted right before he tried to get away from me.

I tightened my grasp.

My brother stilled, following my gaze to the coffee shop instead.

The street cutting between us and our destination was narrow enough that, when the crowd momentarily parted, the shop windows perfectly reflected the two of us.

With his light-blond hair curling at the temples, bright-blue eyes, and light skin, Sisu blended in with the other pedestrians remarkably well. Despite the fact that he'd insisted on wearing shorts along with his heavy boots and oversized thick wool socks. I told him that shorts weren't worn in the autumn by humans, but he'd remained unconvinced. Apparently, he liked his knees to be able to breathe.

I, on the other hand, stuck out more than I'd intended. While Sisu took after his father, my own skin tone was a lighter version of my mother's golden tan, and currently darkened after spending months in the summer sun. The unruly medium-brown hair currently brushing my shoulders and my golden-hazel eyes were also slightly lighter versions of my mother's. My knees were purposefully hidden under thin black tights. They had no need to breathe.

I touched the collar of the sweater I'd paired with my favorite brown plaid skirt. The sleeves were long enough that I had to continually resist the urge to push them up, because doing so would expose the short daggers I wore strapped to my forearms. Those daggers would be masked from casual sight by my magic, but being cautious was how all dragons—and most other magic users for that matter—walked through the world mostly unremarked.

The colorful yoke of the sweater was knitted in the Fair Isle style. My historical and cultural research had indicated that such a textile would be commonplace in Norway.

My out-of-date research.

I hadn't yet seen another person wearing such a sweater. Which only served to feed into my low-level discomfort.

Even though I understood that magic—or fate or destiny, specifically—often moved as it willed without regard to careful planning, I still didn't like being unprepared.

A breeze stirred my already unmanageable hair, coming out of nowhere. I turned into the kiss of the wind, acknowledging it. It shifted to whisper around my knees, then ankles, before abating. I glanced down as a blue flower with white sepals settled on the toe of my brown boot.

Not a breeze.

Magic.

Specifically, the manner in which my own magic occasionally manifested.

I tucked Infinity under my other arm, bending down to retrieve what I was fairly certain was a completely out-of-season blossom. A delicate spring bloom more at home in the mountains, I guessed. The scent of honey tickled my senses, then was gone a moment after I smelled it.

More magic. Not the natural scent of the flower itself.

"Dusk?" Sisu tugged on my hand as he called my name, then muttered something else I didn't catch.

He was speaking Norwegian, not English.

I shifted my hold on Infinity, tucking the slightly hairy stem of the blue blossom between my forefinger and middle finger. I would identify the flower later. But for now, I knew I was where I was meant to be. My magic had told me so.

"Sorry?"

"Hot chocolate?" Sisu repeated in Norwegian. "With whipped cream and a shot of aquavit?"

I was fairly certain a five-year-old human wasn't allowed to drink aquavit, but I'd have to look at the menu before I had enough leverage to rule it out as an option for him.

"Let's go see," I said, speaking in English. I wasn't fluent in Norwegian yet, though I could translate just about any language in written form just by looking at it long enough. Or I could have pulled the correct Norwegian from my connection to Infinity, with perfect pronunciation. I had fed my personal archive multiple dictionaries in anticipation of this trip, but communing with Infinity in that fashion always left me a little nauseated. So, like Sisu, I'd memorized the phrases I thought I might need ahead of time, even though English was spoken extensively in Norway.

Sisu made an attempt to haul me across the street, startling me enough that I was forced to dig my heels into the cobblestones, throwing all my weight back to stop him.

My brother grunted, his nose hovering only a hand's width away from the steady flow of pedestrians laden with shopping bags, coffee cups, and mobile devices.

"Could have made it," he protested.

"Wait for a break in the flow. We don't want to hurt anyone," I said patiently, though holding him back was getting more difficult every day. That was what happened when your five-year-old brother was the child of a guardian dragon while you were just a lowly twenty-five-year-old archivist, still seventy-five years from her majority—aka the threshold that marked adulthood among the dragons.

Carefully weaving through a break in the pedestrians, I pulled Sisu with me across the street.

Sure, I was the Archivist of the Modern World. A lofty title. But it was such a junior position that all it had come with was Infinity. No books, no artifacts, no established library or archive to curate.

Infinity was powerful. I had spent the two years since I'd claimed my personal archive feeding it with all the history and literature that the library at home would yield, plus whatever I could order from Books, Tomes, and Other Publications, or purchase while on other trips. Though before she'd left on her current collection,

Mom usually got to the more interesting books that Oliver Anderson had on offer in London before I could.

But I wanted more.

I had something to prove.

The interior of the coffee shop was a sensory delight. The scent of coffee and sugar hung in the air. Quiet but peppy music played underneath a murmur of polite, engaged conversation. And artwork occupied every vertical surface—black and white nature photographs, mixed media on canvas, and small statues of twisted metal on floating shelves, all of it stark against the white walls.

The thick-edged black-laminate tables were all full of customers, grouped as jean- and sweater-clad duos or trios, or sitting alone, bent over laptops or tablets or phones along the narrow, tall table that fronted the shop.

I wanted a seat by the wall in the corner, so as to be mostly hidden from casual glance on two sides. Content to wait, I joined the short line at the counter.

Sisu instantly plastered himself to the glass enclosure holding pastries, cookies, and sandwiches, as well as juice and water. Each item was carefully labeled in Norwegian and English.

The woman in line behind us swallowed a smile at Sisu's antics. She looked away as I snagged the top of my brother's hoodie and tugged him back gently.

"What does the menu tell you?" I asked quietly, directing Sisu's attention above the counter. The main menu was painted in white block letters on a blackboard that backed the entire workspace. "About the hot chocolate?"

My brother nodded his head, but was still distracted by the display case. "See the little cards? The treats have all been indexed!"

The woman behind us laughed quietly.

That was better than her being upset or mean, presumably. But the reaction—drawing any attention from a human—made me uncomfortable. I still couldn't feel anyone or anything magical in nature in the area, though, other than Infinity now tucked into my backpack and Sisu at my side. My usual range was about three kilometers, even in a city surrounded by technology.

Though a number of Adepts, mostly witches and shapeshifters, made their homes in Oslo, the people in the coffee shop had no idea that magic wielders such as Sisu and myself even existed. Or magical objects like Infinity. And every single Adept, including myself, was tasked with keeping the magical world a secret from the nonmagicals.

I wasn't certain how much longer the Adept remaining a secret from the humans would be possible, though, as fast as technology and science were advancing. Which was one of the main reasons I was going to try to access the World Wide Web with Infinity. Perhaps even forge a connection between the humans' technology and the magical archive.

Or at least that was the explanation I'd give when I got caught.

Because getting caught was highly likely.

But if I was being honest with myself, feeling useless—especially without Mom's guidance and her relentless focus on my training—was making me restless. And possibly rash.

The fact that Sisu and I were in Oslo, not London or Paris where we could have more easily blended in, was a rational choice, though. Not only was it a shorter trip, but also more easily…contained.

Not that anything was going to go wrong.

"Hot chocolate." Sisu gestured toward the menu, speaking in Norwegian. "Milk, not dark chocolate. With sprinkles. And a peanut butter and chocolate chip cookie." He pointed to the row of exceedingly large cookies directly before him.

"What kind of sprinkles?" I asked, teasing. I was somewhat surprised he hadn't asked for the krumkaker cookies—traditional paper-thin wafer cookies baked on a decorative iron and rolled while still hot—which we'd read about while researching our trip. But they were far less substantial than the peanut butter and chocolate chip, so size probably won over tradition in Sisu's mind.

"Rainbow," Sisu said, switching to English. His expression was deeply serious.

We shuffled forward in line. My brother momentarily pressed against my leg, bracing himself on my hip. His touch lingered longer than necessary, dropping to play with the hem of my sweater, then falling away.

I hadn't thought…

Sisu was always so confident, but he'd never been surrounded by so many humans before. I hadn't fully anticipated how he might react.

I loved Sisu to death. But truth be told, the last eleven months had left me feeling more and more like my brother's babysitter than his sister. And if I was being honest with myself—even if only in my own head—Mom's extended absence was beginning to scare me.

Not that I was afraid for her. But I was actually starting to worry that I wasn't enough for my little brother.

More and more, the months we'd spent alone together while I focused on training—and on waiting for a more exciting position to open up—was forcing me to wonder whether Sisu might need more than I could offer him as a surrogate parent. And how soon that might become an issue.

"Would you like to order?" I asked as we stepped forward.

Sisu shook his head, settling his bright-blue, wide-eyed gaze on the woman behind the counter. She appeared to be about eighteen, with blond curly hair streaked with pink, and a ring piercing her right nostril.

I cleared my throat, running the proper Norwegian through in my head.

"I speak English," the cashier said.

Oh. Well.

That was disappointing.

"A small—"

Sisu stomped on my foot.

Hard.

Ignoring my crushed toes, I corrected myself. "A large milk hot chocolate, a peanut butter and chocolate chip cookie, and a small lemon tea, extra hot with honey. Thank you."

The cashier's fingers began flying over her screen before I'd stopped speaking.

"No treat for you?" Sisu asked. "That looks tasty." He pointed toward a filled donut of some sort, smothered in icing and topped with coconut.

"Skolebrod. School bread!" the cashier exclaimed, suddenly animated. "A sweet bun spiced with cinnamon and cardamom, filled with vanilla custard, then baked. It's glazed and topped with coconut."

"Yes, thank you," I said, even though I didn't like anything overly sweet in general.

I pulled the paper money out of my pocket, glancing at the total on the display as I counted it out. The cashier scooped the small pile up. A drawer slid open under the counter, seemingly of its own accord. Human technology was a certain kind of magic all its own.

Guessing its intent by the sign attached to it, I added a bill to the tip jar next to the register.

The cashier's pause, then a crooked smile, informed me that I'd tipped too much. But I couldn't take it back without looking even more out of place.

"I'll bring it over to you." She nodded toward the seating area at the front of the cafe.

I grabbed Sisu's hood and tried to not look like I was dragging him away. Waiting to have his demands met wasn't a concept a young dragon easily understood.

But without protesting the forced abandonment of his cookie, Sisu surged forward to claim a table. The two-seater perfectly tucked into the corner was in the process of being vacated by a couple in their thirties. The woman was wearing a pretty red sweater—with a Fair Isle pattern on the yoke. Her light-blond hair coiled into curls that barely brushed her shoulders, so unlike my own wild mane that I felt momentarily...frumpy.

She caught me looking at her, then glanced at my own outfit. "Oh, does your grandmother knit?" she asked in English.

In English!

Sigh.

"Um," I responded slowly. My maternal grandmother, Ruth, had died before I was born, having ventured into sixteenth-century China in pursuit of a bashe. The mythological serpent—after going insane and deciding it was a dragon—had become obsessed with reclaiming a pearl that it believed contained a prophecy. Since my grandmother had inadvertently released the creature from a misfiled artifact in her own archive, she'd been responsible for its recapture.

My grandmother's ashes—authenticated, so that my mother could claim her inheritance of the estate—were housed in an ornate urn on the mantel in the library. The pearl was safely housed in the personal collection of the treasure keeper of the guardian dragons, where all the exceedingly dangerous artifacts were stored. Pulou, the treasure keeper—aka the guardian dragon who oversaw all the dragon archivists—had personally returned my grandmother's remains.

The fact that the pearl even existed—never mind the prophecy, which was a separate thing altogether—was knowledge that wasn't mine to collect. Not yet. But the family library sometimes yielded things to my touch that it shouldn't, including personal family journals. And my mother hadn't caught me digging through them.

Not yet.

The woman was staring at me, her eyes widening as my silence discomforted her.

I touched the neckline of my sweater. "It's vintage."

"Oh!" She smiled broadly. "Good find."

She meant it was a good thrift-store find. But I had actually excavated the sweater from my mother's wardrobe, deeming it perfect for my attempt to blend in. Though the sweater was old enough that I'd had to bargain to get the preservation spell on it removed. The brownies who were in charge of the estate really didn't like their collections being disturbed. Of course, they also had a habit of preemptively preserving items, tucking them away for safekeeping before their owners were actually done using them.

I smiled, nodding, and the couple finally walked away, weaving through the other tables toward the exit. All the other seats were full.

A few adults still waiting to sit glared at Sisu as he carefully slung his pack across the seat back, mimicking the other customers and those who had jackets similarly slung. I raised my chin and glared back.

Anyone who might have been peeved about a five-year-old stealing a seat looked away.

I might not be the armor-wearing, sword-wielding type of dragon, but that didn't mean I'd let anyone throw shade at my baby brother.

And yes, I'd researched the modern etymology of 'throwing shade.' It had come up while I was research-ing 'texting' and 'social media' during a trip to London six months before, where I'd noticed that almost all the humans had been attached to some form of technology. As they were now in the coffee shop. I'd been aware of computers and such my entire life, of course, but it had been on that London trip that I'd first gotten the idea of trying to download the Internet into Infinity. Hence the research, though it had seriously bored Zeke.

The reminder of how awkward it was to source any modern-day history that couldn't be ordered from a bookstore while on the estate—where technology gen-erally didn't work—made me realize that I'd forgotten to ask for the cafe's Wi-Fi password.

I turned back to the counter, but spotted the pass-word jotted on the bottom of the menu board right in front of me. PASSORD. I narrowed my eyes, and courtesy of my unique magic, the letters shifted into English. The password was…'password.' Ironic. And highly amusing.

I joined Sisu at the table. His feet didn't touch the ground. He met my gaze as I slid into the seat across from him, grinning and bobbing his head as I tugged off my backpack. He held his hands clasped over the small black leather notebook he'd retrieved from his pack, just like Mom did over her own personal archive.

Sisu couldn't yet claim the words he painstakingly wrote in his book. He couldn't feed it to build his own archive. He might never be able to do so. His power—and possible destiny—most likely lay in another direction. I often wondered if our mother had considered that when she'd invited a guardian into her bed.

Dragons didn't breed easily. Guardians, even less so. And they certainly didn't interbreed with other Adept. They simply held too much magic.

We. We held too much magic, too much power.

Of course, Mom might have been simply motivated by a desire for pleasure and companionship. As she might still be even now. And I knew the feeling, of course. But I'd had Mistress Brightshire, the head brownie of our household, brew me her infallible birth control tisane every six months since I was sixteen, the same year I'd decided to seduce one of the other trainees at a summer camp I'd attended.

My first crush had wielded a broadsword with far more skill than any of his personal appendages. And 'seduce' was a massive overstatement.

I had come face-to-face with Sisu's father only six times since he was born. Jiaotu, the guardian of Northern Europe. But it was possible that Mom and he met elsewhere more frequently. Perhaps in the guardian nexus. Or in Giza, where Mom oversaw the entire magical collection housed at the Grand Egyptian Museum. Well, the entire collection in a subsection of that museum, hidden from the humans but nearby just in case the main museum acquired anything that needed to be relocated. Quickly. Before it spelled, maimed, or killed someone.

It had been six months since Jiaotu had last collected Sisu for a weekend visit. That had been when I'd gone to London with Zeke, coming back with a box full of books to find the house still empty. Sisu had walked through the front door unaccompanied two weeks later.

Dragons didn't have a strong grasp of the concept of time, and guardians even less so. Moreover, walking in and out of pocket dimensions, where time often slipped, really didn't help.

We hadn't seen Mom in over eleven months. Three hundred and fifty-one days, to be exact.

"Well?" my brother asked, still grinning.

Smiling back at him, I unzipped my backpack and handed him the tablet. He crouched on the wooden seat of the chair as he powered the tablet up, then hunched over it, fixated on the black screen.

I placed Infinity on the table, opening the thick book to a random blank page and carefully placing the wildflower I was still carrying onto it. Once more, the scent of honey filtered up to me, and I smiled, acknowledging the gift.

Infinity's pages appeared blank. But I could recall any bit of knowledge I'd personally fed into the archive with just a well-formed thought and a brush of my fingers. No one could read Infinity but me. It was the same for all archivists, including Mom, which was why all of us often maintained separate journals that were meant to be passed down through generations.

Because when I died—as when any archivist died—my personal archive would cease to exist as well. Infinity would cease to exist. And any knowledge or object within the archive that hadn't been properly sorted and stored elsewhere would be lost.

I closed Infinity, pressing the flower between its pages. It would be held there, like the other flowers and leaves I pressed within the archive. Unlike the other objects and books I fed into Infinity, which were transported to my personal shelves in the small section of the library my mother had designated for me.

I still wasn't quite certain what was behind that discrepancy. I only knew it had something to do with the magic that brought the flora to me in the first place. It was a unique function of my personal magic that I hadn't figured out yet. The power of archivists wasn't always the same. Or so my mother kept assuring me.

But if I wanted to find the blue blossom again, for whatever reason I might decide I needed it, I knew that all I had to do was request the specific flower or leaf, and Infinity would reopen to the pages it was pressed between.

I kept my left hand on Infinity, slowly scanning the seating area. It wasn't that I thought anyone might try to snatch the ornate leather book from me—given that it was unlikely that any of them could even see it, with all the robust magic it held. But because Infinity was sometimes ... fickle. It might decide it wanted a different view—and start moving of its own accord.

I hadn't mentioned that possible glitch to anyone else yet. It had only started since my mother had been gone. And Zeke would just freak out, as he did with anything out of the ordinary. That was with the understanding that 'ordinary' for a dragon archivist was completely extraordinary for the rest of the magical world. And probably outright ridiculous for the humans.

I was actively choosing to believe that Infinity's quirks were simply a case of a still-incomplete bonding.

For now.

Sisu furrowed his brow, navigating the software preprogrammed into the tablet—touching the little icons reverently. Likely mimicking my own gestures from when we'd discussed the plan on the train.

He'd wanted to access the Wi-Fi en route, but I'd been concerned about doing so. Magic and technology didn't mix well under normal circumstances. And neither Sisu or I would be considered even remotely 'normal' on the magical scale. Sisu even more so than me, though he was the younger by twenty years.

Add in a train moving at high speed, even if we hadn't been that near the engines or the electronics that ran everything, and, well...

I might have been prepared to take responsibility for my actions under the guise of the modern world being my purview, my actual job title and everything. But I wasn't interested in looking like an idiot at the same time. And accidentally derailing a high-speed train would draw far too much attention, especially if I had Sisu with me.

My brother hissed excitedly when a window opened on the tablet screen, prompting him to input the Wi-Fi password. But he hesitated uncharacteristically, rubbing his hands on the tops of his thighs, then pushing the tablet back toward me.

I typed in the password to access the coffee shop's network.

Sisu knelt on his chair, leaning over the table as I typed into the browser window:

WWW.GOOGLE.COM

A person stepped up to our table, holding a tray. Not the cashier. He had dark-blond hair, slightly tanned skin, and multiple metal-studded leather bracelets on each of his wrists.

Sisu shoved the tablet, his notebook, and Infinity to the side. I winced at the slight dent that appeared in the wall as a result, but the server didn't seem to notice as he placed down our drinks and treats.

My brother immediately slurped all the melting whipped cream from the top of his hot chocolate, getting it all in a single mouthful. I hoped he hadn't just inhaled the sprinkles.

I opened my mouth to chastise him, but a gentle laugh from the server and the people at the nearest table let me know that no one else objected to his behavior, so I let it go.

"Thank you," I murmured to the server.

Still grinning, he stepped away without another word, picking up some dirty dishes as he moved through the tightly packed tables.

"Nothing is happening," Sisu said. Whipped cream topped one half of his upper lip.

I gestured toward my own face. He tried to lick the cream from his lip, unsuccessfully.

"Nothing's happening," he said again, reaching for the tablet.

"I haven't placed it properly yet," I said, rearranging the items on the table. Setting Infinity directly before me, I shifted my lemon tea to one side and the treats into the center of the available space.

Sisu crammed easily half of the peanut butter and chocolate chip cookie into his mouth, already eyeing my custard-filled bun. Now halved, the cookie was still larger than his hand.

I set the tablet on top of Infinity, lining up its metal-cased edges to the golden-etched edge of the archive. The browser window was still open to Google.

Nothing happened.

It was possible I needed to type something into the empty search window to trigger the connection.

Sisu grunted, dissatisfied. His mouth was full of the other half of the cookie.

"Wait for it," I murmured.

Still nothing happened.

I picked up the tablet, flipping Infinity open and setting the device down on the first blank page.

Then I waited. Again.

Nothing happened.

"Put it in," Sisu hissed, spraying chunks of cookie across the table. He clamped his hand over his mouth, momentarily embarrassed.

I shook my head, most of my attention on the tablet. I should have tested my theory before dragging us all the way into Oslo, but there had been no way to truly do so closer to home.

Okay, that wasn't entirely true.

Every small village in Norway had Wi-Fi. And Bergen, where we'd caught the high-speed train, was a city in its own right.

But I had wanted the trip. The train ride. I liked the planning, the sense of adventure. And for too long now, our days at the estate had been a little…empty. Just the two of us at home training, studying, in between visits from Zeke or one of the apprentices of our sword master, Branson, showing up to test us.

Sisu finished chewing, then repeated, "Put it in."

"Don't say that," I muttered.

He took a large swig of his hot chocolate. His lips pursed in a grimace, his face reddening like he was absorbing the heat.

"Put it in," he insisted again, gasping.

"Stop saying that," I hissed.

"Put it in, put it in," he chanted, slowly sliding his fingertips toward my custard-filled bun. As if I couldn't see him moving. "Put it in."

I flushed. I was going to have to give Sisu a reason to stop repeating himself. My little brother always needed a reason. "That means something else. Stop it."

"You put things in your archive all the time." Sisu snagged the edge of my plate and tried dragging it to him.

I tugged the plate out of his reach.

He grimaced.

Yes. I still moved faster than him. Though not by much.

"It means what else?" He clasped his hot chocolate in both hands, taking tiny consecutive sips this time.

"It's a sexual innuendo."

"Like how babies are made?"

"Yes." My cheeks flushed. I was painfully aware that we were surrounded by humans, though none of the other customers were paying the least bit of attention to us.

A wide grin swamped Sisu's face.

Oh no. That bit of information was about to backfire on me.

"Put it in," he chanted quietly, still sipping his hot chocolate. "Put it in."

I sighed. Nothing was happening with the tablet. So I tugged Infinity and the tech into my lap, then turned toward the wall. I pulled my backpack off the chair, making it appear as if I were looking for something within it.

I flipped Infinity, opening the back cover instead of the front. Whenever I fed handwritten words or previously written knowledge that wasn't mine to collect into my archive, I did so through the front. But any magical item or artifact I was actively collecting was absorbed into Infinity through the back, then automatically stored on my personal shelves in the library.

Infinity usually scanned each object as it passed through its pages, storing as much information as it could retrieve at the same time. So the same might work with the tablet and its connection to the World Wide Web via the coffee shop's Wi-Fi.

I rested the corner of the tablet on the archive's blank, rough-edged, thick linen page.

About five centimeters of the tablet slipped into the archive. I kept a tight hold on Infinity and the tech. Energy shifted as the archive became aware that I was offering it something interesting.

That energy tugged on the tablet.

I kept hold of it. "No," I whispered. "Just taste, then access the data." I allowed my own energy to pool in and around my archive. I didn't usually need to add my own magic to the process, not since I'd tied Infinity to me in the first place. But feeding it tech was unorthodox. Literally. Many dragons subscribed to a multitude of religions, occasionally at the same time. Some had no need of faith at all. But I fell somewhere in the middle. Believing in a higher power made sense to me. I needed the comfort of the idea that some being was more powerful, more knowledgeable, than myself.

But I didn't believe in any god. Rather, magic and spirit and pure energy were my religion.

Images started to flicker on the tablet screen.

Sisu hissed excitedly.

I met his grin with one of my own. It was working!

Infinity wound more and more of its energy around the tablet. Trying to claim it. But I held it firmly. If the archive sucked the tablet into its depths, then the connection to the Wi-Fi wouldn't hold. And presumably the tablet would be fried in the process.

More windows, text, and photos flashed open on the screen, searing themselves into my brain as Infinity absorbed the information. I had to quickly look away or risk getting a massive headache.

Sisu was eating my custard-filled bun.

"Hey!"

He shrugged, then grinned, displaying a mouthful of chewed bread.

Infinity yanked on the tablet.

Hard.

I lost hold. The metal that housed the tech was smooth, and it momentarily slid from my grasp. I managed to grab the corner again just before it disappeared. "No, Finny," I hissed. "We discussed this. It doesn't work if—"

The archive swallowed the tablet completely, getting the tips of my fingers along with it. My hand went numb, energy streaking through nerves, muscles, and bones. I jerked away, shaking my hand.

I stared down at the blank page. Blinking at it. Like an idiot.

Damn it.

Sisu's mouth had dropped open, his eyes wide. "I didn't see nothing."

"Anything. You didn't see anything."

"That too." He frowned, fingers sticky from my sweet bun. "Do you have another one?"

"No." I sighed, glancing around. No one appeared to be watching us. No one appeared to have noticed anything untoward.

"Why didn't you buy two?" Sisu hissed.

Infinity vomited up the tablet. I caught it before it hit me in the chin. The screen was black.

Then my archive went inert in my lap.

All its magic sucked inward, and then...and then...it just felt like...like...

Like a regular book.

Fear tingled down my spine, pooling in my belly with a heavy sense of dread. My mind went numb. I...I had hurt Infinity.

I'd...ruined Infinity?

A murmur ran through the customers at the front counter, perched with their laptops and other devices. Then a series of quiet questions ran through the seating area. In Norwegian.

I closed Infinity, flipping the archive, then laying my hand on it so it could feed me the translation. The murmurs rose. People began glancing around.

Infinity didn't respond to my touch or my unvoiced request.

"The...connection..." Sisu said, struggling to translate. "The...Wi-Fi? It dropped?"

Ah, shit.

A few customers abandoned their seats, moving toward the counter with questions. Dread over what I might have done to my archive continued to numb me from the inside out, but I quickly tucked Infinity and the tablet into my backpack, reaching for my ignored tea.

"Nothing else has happened," I said, flicking my gaze around the room over the rim of my ceramic mug. "It should be fine. Just act—"

Something crackled within the wall next to us. Something it was unlikely the humans could hear. But I could.

Sisu shifted slightly out of his chair, eyeing the electrical outlet set into the wall at table height so that people could charge their—

The overhead lights flickered.

Then went out.

The murmurs increased. Not panicked. Just questioning.

Abandoning my tea, I shouldered my pack and reached for Sisu's hand.

He grabbed the last of the custard-filled bun along with some paper napkins, his notebook, and his backpack.

Sliding between humans before they had a chance to see us pass, we swiftly exited the coffee shop.

From the sidewalk, we watched as the power winked out in store after store, building after building. Though there weren't as many as before, other pedestrians paused to watch, then to question the cascading power outage.

Evening had encroached on the city during the time we'd been in the coffee shop. The sun had already started to set, far earlier than I'd anticipated. It had been utterly stupid for me to wield any sort of magic in the hour of my birth without focused intent.

I mean, obviously, I had been focused and working with intent. But I was unusually powerful during the transition from day into night—another oddity in how my magic manifested. Most dragons were simply powerful all the time. My mother blamed the witches who had overseen my birth for that peculiarity.

Those same witches had named me for the hour of my birth in an elaborate ceremony. Dusk, they called me.

All right, maybe 'blamed' was too harsh a word. Mostly, as when I questioned her about any of the oddities in my power, my mother just shrugged and changed the subject. Or she loaned me a book.

And yes, I knew when I was being deliberately distracted. But no sane archivist ever turned down a new book.

Damn. Damn.

Sisu bounced up and down, grinning madly. "Did we do that?"

I tugged him to the left, quickly stepping into a narrow side road with cars parked on either side of the street. The buildings above and ahead of us had gone dark as well. We wouldn't be visiting the bookstore. But from my memorization of the tourist map, I knew we could access the next street over and loop back to the train station.

Out of sight of the coffee shop entrance, I paused to help Sisu organize his backpack and secure it on his back. He wrapped the remainder of the custard-filled bun in the paper napkins and offered it to me, patting my cheek with a sticky hand.

I sighed, crouching so he could tuck the bun in my own backpack. I knew Sisu would eat it later, but it was sweet of him to try to console me.

I still couldn't feel any magic from Infinity. Not even a whisper. The dread that had hardened like lead in my belly was making me sick.

Magic bloomed ahead of us. An intense pinpoint of power that wiped every thought from my mind.

The pinpoint grew, widening.

Sisu clung to my arm.

I straightened, pressing him behind me, needing my arms free. He fisted his hands in my sweater, peering around my hip. If we had to run, he would climb up onto my back—a contingency factoring in Sisu's youth, which we'd practiced numerous times during our dual training sessions with the sword master's apprentices.

But dragons rarely ran from anything. Toward things? Most definitely. That characteristic was practically written into our DNA, our function within the magical world.

The pinpoint of power welled. Glowing golden and bright, it spread outward like an upright whirlpool. The power made my bones ache, but I recognized it.

A portal.

Specifically, a guardian dragon portal. Just like the ones Jiaotu used when he visited Sisu. The power signature was unmistakable. As was to be expected when dealing with any of the nine most powerful beings in existence. Or in this dimension, at least.

This was a power we couldn't evade.

This, we couldn't fight.

"They know!" Sisu cried. "How can they know already?"

My heart was hammering in my chest, the dread washing away as adrenaline flooded my system. "If...if it was...if plugging Infinity into the Internet was wrong...or bad for the world somehow, the guardians would have stopped me ahead of time, so...it's going to be okay."

No one crossed through the portal to confront us. It simply hung there, just wide enough to walk through. Specifically, for two people to walk through hand in hand, if one was much smaller than the other.

And technically, only dragons could cross through guardian magic.

We were being summoned.

To the nexus? Or by a specific guardian?

I crouched down, pulling Sisu in front of me.

My brother stared at me with wide eyes, silently panicking.

I never should have brought him with me. He could have stayed on the estate grounds by himself for a day, even if it had turned into overnight. I should have trusted him to do that, should have trusted the brownies to watch over him. But with Mom gone, I hadn't wanted to worry him.

I never wanted him to have to worry about losing me as well.

I ran my fingers through Sisu's hair, almost as unruly as mine. One of the only characteristics we both shared with Mom. Wetting my thumb with saliva, I made an attempt to get some of the stickiness off his face, then brushed crumbs from his hoodie before zipping it up partway. "Speak only if you are spoken to. Keep your answers short. Be truthful."

Sisu nodded, lips thin and pale with fear.

I pressed a kiss to his temple, whispering, "I'm sorry."

He nodded, flicking his gaze to the portal. Then he narrowed his eyes defiantly.

I quashed a grin as I straightened, squaring my shoulders and lifting my chin.

Dragons didn't tremble. Dragons didn't beg for forgiveness or break under pressure. Dragons walked through magical maelstroms, quashing demon uprisings and thwarting invasions before stopping off for dim sum for breakfast. In Shanghai.

Well, guardian dragons did that sort of thing.

I just recorded it all.

But still, the same genes and power ran in my veins, and even more so in Sisu's blood.

I glanced around us. Humans might not be able to see the portal itself, but they would certainly see us disappear into it. Thankfully, the side street was quiet. The buildings nearest to us were still dark. But as I watched, street and apartment lights flickered on a couple of blocks away. Whatever I'd done to knock out the electricity apparently wasn't permanent, or even long lasting.

Well, that was going to be a lot easier to justify. Or maybe just not mention at all?

I took my brother's hand, and together we walked into the portal.

CHAPTER TWO

THOUGH I WAS A DRAGON, I HAD NEVER ACTUALLY travelled by portal. I had never even seen one prior to five years ago. But I had felt the power of multiple portals since Sisu was born, because his father was a guardian, and portals were everyday transport for the nine most powerful beings in the world.

The golden funnel—called forth by the treasure keeper, who was the only one of the nine who could create the portals—cut through space and ignored time. At least as far as I knew. Portals were thus the quickest way for a guardian to get to the site of something untoward, such as a massive demon summoning. Or for Jiaotu to visit Sisu.

If I were the treasure keeper, I expected I'd be pretty bored transporting the others around on command. But that was a unique aspect of Pulou's position, his power. All dragons fulfilled the tasks assigned to them to the absolute best of their abilities, but each of the guardians wielded specific powers beyond the rest of us. And the nine guardians together …? Well, according to myth and legend, the nine demigods held the divided power of a single divine being, so that none was more powerful than the others. But together, they could vanquish anything, anyone. Though it was rare that it took more than one guardian to face down any threat or foe.

Still, since being the absolute best Archivist of the Modern World that I could be—junior position or not—was my second reason for attempting to connect Infinity to the Internet, I certainly wasn't going to be suggesting that any duty was boring. Whether or not it might have been boredom driving me in the first place.

The power fueling and directing the portal thrummed across my skin, digging into my bones. Though not unpleasantly. My footfalls felt solid within the tunnel of golden light, though I knew I stood on magic, not anything solid.

Sisu gripped my hand. I kept my chin raised and my gaze straight ahead, prepared for whatever waited for me.

The golden wash of power released us.

My front foot fell onto a white marble floor.

And suddenly I was in a large round room, staring at gilded pillars, an elaborately painted domed ceiling, and nine ornate doors.

Sisu and I were standing under a large archway directly across from a twin arch, which appeared to lead to more gilded marble corridors.

The room was otherwise empty.

"The nexus," I murmured.

We'd been transported to the seat of power for the guardian dragons, which I recognized instantly from the numerous sketches and written descriptions in the journals of my family members. Each of the nine ornate doors led to a different territory, to portals permanently anchored at multiple points. Locations that were only a thought away. For the guardians, at least.

Sisu was staring at a door decorated in shades of white and gray, carved with the image of a wolf and a raptor flashing viciously long claws and talons. Though it didn't perfectly match the rendering in my Great-Grandfather George's journal, it was unmistakably the door that led to the territories of Jiaotu, the guardian of Northern Europe. Sisu's father.

I found myself wondering if that door had been permanently anchored to our family estate now. Sisu's father had walked through our front door unannounced without disturbing a single ward, multiple times.

I was currently sharing some sketches and stories from the journals with Sisu at bedtime. Heavily edited versions of the stories, anyway. The fact that I could even touch my great-grandfather's journals was another peculiarity of my archivist abilities. George had been the head curator of the guardian nexus library. But though he was currently missing—subsumed into the library itself for a hundred and two years now—he hadn't been officially declared dead yet. Therefore I shouldn't have been able to pull any of the items from his shelves in the family library. But his journals yielded to my touch... albeit with much coaxing and cajoling. Sisu couldn't touch any of the journals, though. Not even after I'd held them.

I took in each of the other doors, trying to place the territories they led to by the carvings that adorned each. The door to Haoxin's North American territory was wooden, perhaps cedar or fir, and carved in an ab-original design. The Western European door, leading to Suanmi's territory, was embossed in fleurs-de-lis cast of yellow gold. And the Asian territories overseen by Chi Wen the far seer were denoted by a red door, carved across the middle with a massive Chinese dragon holding a pearl. It was inlaid with what I thought might have been red jade and gold.

No one greeted us.

The portal had completely dissipated after depositing us in the nexus. And I still had no idea why it had opened for us in the street in the first place, then brought us into the dimensional pocket that was the epicenter of the guardian dragons' power.

Fear, then trepidation, began to pool in my belly. What if we weren't being summoned because I'd fed active technology to Infinity? What if this wasn't about me knocking out the power across what had appeared to be at least three city blocks?

What if something had happened to my mother?

No.

Someone would have come to the estate. As they had when my grandfather, Farhad, had been found petrified in the stacks of the nexus library, likely dead for at least a half-century before he'd been excavated from the Mesopotamian section of the main collection. Cause of death had been recorded as 'unknown,' but was most likely starvation. Archivists could get a little obsessive. And the nexus library had a reputation for wanting to keep anything or anyone that crossed through its stacks.

Items deemed too powerful for any individual archivist to hold were continually sent to the nexus library or the treasure keeper's personal archive. Those books, documents, and artifacts were then occasionally relocated by an archivist who'd gained permission to access the archives or the library. That archivist would often redistribute the book or artifact to one of the other major archival collections throughout the world, making it available to any Adept.

Well, to any Adept who actually knew that the archives existed in the first place, and who then jumped through a ton of hoops to prove they had the right to access the information collected there.

When my mother had taken over for her Uncle Jamal in Giza—he wasn't dead, just not fully functional—she had spent weeks pulling items from the nexus library. Luckily, the library had liked her and allowed her to leave once she was done. Possibly because she was pregnant with Sisu, the child of a guardian, at the time.

It was also lucky for Zeke—because my mother had rescued him from the nexus library during that same collection. When she related the story of finding her great-uncle, who had been missing for over three hundred years and therefore officially declared dead, my mother talked about how the library had placed the book that held Zeke—a spelled copy of *The Iliad*—in her hands, even though she specialized in Egyptian artifacts.

After he'd been brought forth from the book, Zeke swore that he'd never even set foot in the guardian nexus or its library. But occasionally, when an archivist died, entire collections were absorbed into the guardians' library. As had been the case with my Great-Grandmother Diana's personal collection. Zeke's sister.

"Is it Mom?" Sisu asked quietly, firmly gripping my hand.

I shook my head in quick denial, then remembered that my brother didn't need platitudes. He needed information.

Because information was power.

More so than any other weapon.

"No," I said, forcing confidence into my tone. "When Grandfather Farhad was found dead, they sent someone to the house to inform Mom."

"How old were you?"

"Around your age. Almost six."

He frowned thoughtfully. "Six present years?"

The actual age of some archivists became a little convoluted to track through the centuries. Me, for example. I'd technically been born in the 1950s, due to a misstep my mother had taken in the stacks of the archives of the British Museum in London, where she'd been authenticating an artifact. She had gone into labor, triggered by that inadvertent time slip—and I'd been born a month early, delivered by the Dunkirk coven while Mom was only partially conscious. It had taken her two years to find her way back to the main timeline, with me in tow. So I was born in 1952, time slipped forward with my mother from 1954 to 1998, and was only twenty-five years old in 2021.

And Mom had been gone for eleven months now, and I had no idea if she'd slipped through time again, or…

I shoved the dark thought away. "Yes," I said. "Six present years old."

"Okay." Sisu shifted his feet, loosening his grip on my hand. His earlier wariness was wearing off.

I doubted this was my brother's first time in the guardian nexus, but I hesitated to outright ask him. The question felt too intimate, and I didn't doubt that every word we said was being listened to by someone.

As if to punctuate my point, two simple wooden chairs and a table appeared before one of the large archways across from us, facing into the long, seemingly endless corridor beyond. The small table remained empty for a moment, then was suddenly set with a tiny round teapot, two tiny mugs, and a plate of white jelly-like squares.

Coconut jelly—an Asian dessert.

Sisu dropped my hand, darting forward. He dumped his backpack on the ground beside the chair on the right, then climbed onto it, kneeling and facing back toward me. "Don't let the tea get bitter. You don't like it like that."

I didn't. I wasn't a huge fan of green tea at all, but I had no doubt the blend the guardians favored would be delicious. Which is to say, the blend served by the brownies who moved around us unseen in the nexus.

Sisu hovered his hand over the coconut jelly squares, then blinked at me for permission.

I nodded, crossing to join him. I didn't like having seven of the nine doorways behind me, or the yawning corridor open in front. The two doors on either side of the large archway were barely in my peripheral vision. The dimensions of the nexus felt odd to me, seemingly shifting around us.

As if to prove exactly that point, the doorways switched positions as I settled in the empty chair. Glancing between those doors—the ones I assumed led to the Northern and Western European territories, respectively—I noted as I hadn't before that neither had a knob or a pull or even hinges.

I kept my backpack on, still painfully aware that Infinity remained inert within it. Yes, it was possible that the almost overpowering magic of the nexus might be masking the magical signature of the archive, but my connection to Infinity was strong enough that I should have been able to feel at least a glimmer of energy. I thought about touching the archive to confirm, then hesitated. Out of fear of what I might have done to it.

Apparently, I was a coward. A rash, possibly arrogant coward. And sitting in the nexus, mentally preparing to be taken to task by one of the guardians, was an absolutely terrible time to come to such a personal realization.

Sisu hunched over the tea set between us, carefully pouring tea into one of the cups. It was barely tinted with color, just as I liked it. He set down the blue hand-hewn pot, turning the handle toward me. I picked it up, obliging him by following the Asian tradition of never pouring your own tea, at least not first.

Technically, neither of us were of Asian descent. Neither was Sisu's father, though he bore the name Jiaotu. But the myths that the guardians cloaked themselves in—as demigods who walked the earth—were best interpreted by Chinese mythology. The nexus itself was anchored in an actual temple in Shanghai. One of the doors behind us, likely the one with the red jade and gold dragon, led directly into that city, no portal needed. For a guardian, at least.

Sisu popped one of the coconut-jelly cubes in his mouth and hummed appreciatively. I made a mental note to learn the proper name of the dessert so I could order them in Cantonese the next time we ate in an actual Chinese restaurant.

"I like dim sum," my brother said, seemingly picking a topic at random. Though, more likely, he'd had the dessert with his father after dim sum, and the brownie who was invisibly serving us—and more likely watching over us—must have plucked the idea from his mind. Or perhaps the nexus brownies had served Sisu before and knew what he liked.

A large wooden table appeared before the archway. Its top was scarred and weathered, its thick legs carved in a simple, almost crude fashion. At least compared to all the other ornate, ostentatious decor surrounding us.

I had never seen the table before, but I knew what it represented.

My heart began hammering in my chest, and I had to blink through a sudden faintness that I'd never experienced before.

"Dusk?" Sisu asked. "What's wrong?"

He could hear my heart rate, or perhaps my magic had spiked. I needed to calm down. For multiple reasons. "We're being summoned before the Guardian Council," I said, pleased that my voice was steady, if a little thin.

"But ..." Sisu chewed on his lip.

Yes, I'd also been assuming that we'd been brought to speak to one guardian, most likely Sisu's father. The appearance of the table was well documented, though, including a sketch in my Great-Grandfather George's journals.

I needed to get to my feet. I needed to prove that I deserved to stand before the guardians awaiting us.

Removing my backpack, I stood and crossed to the table. I placed the pack down on it, unzipping it to remove Infinity. The archive still felt inert, and with my chest compressing further, I struggled to stay on task and not mourn what I might have done to it. I pressed my hand to the worn leather cover, desperately hoping just for one moment that this wasn't going to be the last time I'd ever see my archive. Hoping that I'd have a chance to fix whatever I'd done to it.

Because I had a terrible feeling I was about to be demoted.

And I wasn't certain what happened to archivists who were stripped of their positions.

Sisu set his backpack beside mine.

"We can't bring any weapons into the chamber," I said, pushing up the sleeves of my sweater to expose my forearms, and removing the short daggers strapped there. I set the blades on the table beside Infinity, but left the soft leather arm sheaths cinched in place.

Sisu frowned. "Your archive isn't a weapon."

I smiled. The expression felt tight on my face, but I couldn't seem to soften it. I'd never been so scared in my life. Granted, I was only twenty-five and had been mostly trained at home by people who loved me. But still. "It might not have any sharp edges, but it is most definitely a weapon."

"Because of … because of the knowledge you store in it?"

"Partly. But also because it's pure magic. Pure power. A manifestation of my power, do you understand? Next to a guardian we might seem meek, but archivists are powerful as well."

"I know," Sisu said gruffly.

"I'm just starting to build my arsenal," I said. My heart rate settled as I slipped into teaching mode. "But you should see what Mom can retrieve from her archive."

Sisu's eyebrows shot up to his hairline. "You can pull stuff out? Like what? Like the tablet?"

"Sure. But a fried tablet isn't going to help me fight off anyone."

Sisu trailed his fingers over the hilt of one of my daggers. I'd wrapped both in soft, thin leather, preferring a bit of cushioning rather than risking blisters. The blades were platinum, inlaid with gold. A sixteenth birthday present from my mother. Years of practice had honed the daggers with my magic, sharpening them with layers and layers of my power. Just as Infinity was slowly being filled and sharpened.

Unfortunately, the deadliest thing I could currently retrieve from Infinity would be a couple of water imps that I'd relocated to a pond on the estate after I'd discovered them creating chaos in a children's park in the nearby village.

Assuming the archive wasn't dead.

I was still holding out hope that Infinity was simply momentarily inert from having absorbed too much information. Or that it was still in the process of absorbing that information.

The water imps would have been a bad choice anyway. The poor things would have self-combusted simply standing at the very edge of the power effortlessly wielded by a single guardian. And I was most definitely about to meet more than one demigod.

I couldn't think of any other reason that the main council chamber was about to open.

"What about a chimera?" Sisu asked, his tone far too casual.

Mom had a chimera on her personal shelves. It had followed Zeke out of the spelled *Iliad*, and she had contained it. Shelving the magical creature instead of killing it.

On a shelf that neither Sisu or I could access.

Chimeras really couldn't be easily relocated.

"Why?" I asked pointedly.

Sisu shrugged, suddenly not inclined to answer.

I frowned at him. But before I could push him to elaborate, a large set of double doors inlaid with jewels filled the archway before us.

Oh, yes. We'd definitely been summoned by the guardian nine.

I really, really hoped I wasn't about to self-combust myself.

And standing in that moment, barely able to breathe, my unvoiced concerns about my ability to look after Sisu were completely ironic, suddenly ridiculously dependent on what was about to happen behind the jewel-inlaid doors rather than any immaturity on my part.

I couldn't lose my brother.

And he couldn't lose me.

Sisu and I were the youngest in our immediate familial line. And without Mom... well, there really was no one else who could take my brother. Not without tearing him away from his life, from me.

I couldn't imagine Jiaotu being responsible for raising Sisu. The last time they'd had one of their visits, my brother had come back with nightmares that still haunted him.

And Jiaotu didn't have any living family who could help with raising a five-year-old. As with all of the nine, he had literally been stricken from his own family tree when he'd taken on the guardian mantle over two hundred years ago. Who any of the guardians had been in their previous lives fell away when they became one of the nine. The mantle of guardian subsumed the person who accepted it, transforming them completely.

So the nearest blood relations Sisu currently had—in the present and accounted for—were me, Zeke, and Aunt Josephine. After three centuries lost in time, Zeke was barely accustomed to the twenty-first century. He definitely couldn't raise Sisu, or even look after him, until Mom returned. And Aunt Josephine lived in an archive of her own construction in Crete. Meaning she never left it. My mother's sister, elder by a century, Josephine's mind and magic weren't... in tune with raising a child. She'd lose Sisu five minutes after he showed up. Literally.

The doors swung outward, inviting us forward.

I took Sisu's hand, leading him around the table—and leaving Infinity behind for the first time since I'd laid hands on the archive two years before, claiming it as my own.

"I love you," I said, just in case I never got another chance to say it. "I'll always love you, whether I'm by your side or not."

My mother said that to us each time she went on a collection. And other than echoing it back when she said it, I'd never told another person that I loved them.

I looked down at my brother, smiling as broadly and fiercely as I could. And meaning it. I wouldn't appear weak in front of another dragon, let alone however many guardians awaited us. "Ready for our next adventure?"

Sisu squeezed my hand, too hard. I might still be faster than him, but he was rapidly outgrowing me in strength. "Ready."

I lost Sisu from one step to the next. All my senses were overwhelmed by a wash of magic that whited out my sight. One moment I was holding him. And the next, his hand was just gone from mine.

I clenched my hands, barely stopping myself from crying out.

A room resolved around me. Or at least a tiny subsection of it did. The edges remained undefined—an endless vastness of time and space stretched out in all directions around nine ornate chairs situated on a slightly curved, slightly raised dais.

Five of the nine chairs were currently occupied, but overwhelmed by Sisu's sudden disappearance, I focused all my attention on the white-blond, light-skinned male lounging at the end to my right. Though he appeared to be in his early thirties, he'd worn the mantle of Jiaotu for just over two hundred years, making him at least three hundred years old.

I opened my mouth, already snarling a demand.

The guardian of Northern Europe—my brother's father, my mother's lover—flicked his fingers placatingly. "He is in my rooms."

"Did you have to scare him at the same time?" I sneered. My ire was completely uncharacteristic. But then, I'd never had someone I loved torn so effortlessly from my hand, from my care, before.

Jiaotu's light-blue eyes narrowed, flicking momentarily toward the guardian on his right. A woman, her dark-brown hair swept back from her formidable face, dressed in what I was fairly certain was a vintage designer suit, though I wasn't well versed in such things. She appeared to be in her midforties, though she was well over six hundred years old.

Suanmi.

I'd never met the fire breather. But thankfully, Great-Grandfather George had sketched each guardian as he'd met them while he'd been the nexus library's head curator. Because above all else an archivist needed to know, we first specialized in our own heritage.

I cleared my throat, remembering to dip my head as I reined in my anger. Well, my fear masquerading as anger. At losing my hold on Sisu.

One day, the guardians would call my brother into service. And I would likely never see him again.

One or two hundred years from now, barring any disastrous incidents—because the guardians weren't actually immortal, just exceedingly hard to kill—it was possible I'd be facing a Guardian Council that contained my brother. Except he would no longer be Sisu. He'd be one of the nine, adopting his predecessor's name, wielding their magic. He would be transformed into the root of my bloodline, my power, my species. No longer my younger brother.

Wiped from my family tree.

But never from my memory.

I remembered almost everything—anything I read, saw, or touched.

So even when magic, when destiny, took him from me, Sisu would always be mine.

But still, I bowed my head, hands clenched at my sides. Because at only five years of age and with my mother missing, Sisu couldn't lose me today.

"I understand that what happened at the coffee shop might have been…out of the ordinary," I said. "But you made me the Archivist of the Modern World! I was just doing my job! And clearly the power was coming back on just as we left."

"What coffee shop?" Jiaotu asked.

I shut my mouth. Far too late, of course. But apparently, I was still angry. And doing a terrible job of concealing it.

To my far left, someone snorted—Haoxin, the youngest of the guardians. No one else spoke. I dropped my gaze to my boots, furiously trying to figure out how to backtrack.

Haoxin, the guardian of North America, looked quite different from my great-grandfather's sketch. Definitely younger. Though guardians had some control over their appearance and the rate at which they aged, she had taken on the mantle of Haoxin only in the last century. It was her mother who'd been Haoxin before her.

"Confirm your identity," Suanmi demanded, letting me off the hook. For the moment, at least. She spoke with a French accent—European, not of the Americas. Power rode her words in a way that sounded deadly. Or at least it might have been, if I was some random dragon who'd walked through their portal by mistake.

I wasn't.

"Dusk," I said, "of the Zhi archivists—"

"Named by witches," Jiaotu sneered, cutting off the rest of my formal introduction. "During that … incident."

That incident. My mother being sucked through the stacks of the British Museum archives, dropping into 1952, and barely being conscious during my birth. That incident?

"Oh!" the dark-haired, olive-skinned guardian situated at the center of the curved dais exclaimed, as if just tuning into the conversation. "You're Trissa's child."

Bixi. She of All Forms.

Currently the third-oldest guardian, Bixi was actually a distant blood relation—my Great-Great-Great-Grandmother. She had taken on the mantle of the guardian while unknowingly pregnant with my Great-Great-Grandfather Darius. It was still the only recorded instance of an unborn child surviving the onslaught of power that came with the transference of the magic of a guardian, and it gifted Darius with an unusually long life, among other unique traits. My mother first met Darius over breakfast when she was only my age, and as far as anyone in the family knew for certain, he was still alive.

Ironically, though I knew practically everything there was to know about my mother's family, I knew practically nothing about my own father or his family, other than his name—Rubert—and that he was an archivist out of his own present time. My mother had loved him so much that, for some as yet unarticulated reason, she'd concealed her pregnancy from her family. Technically Sisu was my half-brother, though that distinction had never seemed important.

I dropped my gaze. "Yes, guardian," I said. "My mother is on a collection right now."

I assumed that Bixi's awareness of my mother came from her role as the head curator for the Giza archives. Egypt was in the guardian of Northern Africa's territory, after all. Mom was the current specialist for all Egyptian history, a position she'd been appointed to just over six years ago. Bixi likely had no idea of any distant blood connection between us.

I glanced at Jiaotu, suddenly putting something together that I hadn't before. Mom had taken over for her paternal uncle, Jamal, right before she'd gotten pregnant with Sisu. So she had probably met the guardian of Northern Europe while perusing the library in the nexus. She'd been given access with her new position, 'to see if the guardians were holding anything for which she could provide a more suitable home.' At least that was how she phrased it. Other dragons were less generous when discussing the so-called proclivities that were second nature to an archivist like Mom. Or me. They called us hoarders. Gatekeepers.

"Your mother is on a collection? Still?" Jiaotu asked, seemingly thrown. Since most guardians didn't have a great grasp of time, and I didn't actually know how often he and my mother even saw each other, I was surprised he'd asked for clarification.

I nodded slightly.

Bixi leaned forward, blinking her dark eyes at me. They were heavily lined in kohl. Her dark hair was swept back from her face, and golden chains of various thicknesses were layered over her collarbone, wrists, and ankles. But instead of the elaborate toga I had often seen her pictured in, she was wearing wide-legged linen pants and a golden netted tank top layered over a white tank top. "She's seeking something interesting?"

I bobbed my head more obligingly. "I would think so, guardian. She's been gone for eleven months."

"Months..." Bixi murmured, as if the concept eluded her. And since she was over eight hundred years old, perhaps it did. She lounged back, falling silent.

To my far left, Haoxin huffed, then muttered, "Why is She of All Forms here again?" Envy-worthy golden waves of hair danced around the guardian of North America's shoulders. She was wearing a blue silk dress and strappy gold sandals. Catching my eye, she winked, then folded her legs underneath her. The chair expanded to accommodate her shift in position.

"Quorum," the older guardian on Haoxin's left muttered. I let my gaze shift to him, finally. Trying my best to look deferential. Pulou. The treasure keeper. His massive frame was draped in a huge fur coat, spanning from his shoulders to his ankles. He was wearing faded black jeans, a black T-shirt, and worn black-laced boots. His hands rested on the arms of his chair, legs crossed.

He didn't wear any jewelry or display any weapons of power. Which was highly ironic, because as the treasure keeper, Pulou was not only the overseer of the system of portals—including the one that had brought Sisu and me to the nexus—but was in charge of housing and guarding reportedly epic amounts of magical treasure.

Literally, he was the dragon who oversaw the hoard. And though we'd never personally met, Pulou was also the overseer of the archivists.

"And how has Sisu been?" Jiaotu asked.

I blinked. "Fine, guardian. I mean, he misses—"

"Are we done with the pleasantries?" Suanmi sighed, completely dignified in her detached weariness. "I can't lounge around here all day for some...scheme." That last word was uttered as if it was the absolute worst thing she'd ever been forced to say. Or to participate in.

"It was your idea," Haoxin said.

Suanmi shrugged, the gesture both elegant and utterly dismissive. "It wasn't I who demanded it be brought before the council."

Jiaotu grimaced. "As she has already proclaimed rather...thoroughly, Dusk is currently the Archivist of the Modern World. She has been in that position for only two—"

Suanmi flicked her fingers. "A nothing position. Especially for this child."

I let the 'child' comment roll off me without twitching a muscle. I was back on my best behavior.

Suanmi smirked. "You all can feel the power she wields as well as I can."

"The fact that we can feel it so acutely should remind us all that Dusk is seventy-five years away from her majority." Jiaotu pronounced each word precisely. It was the most vivid display of emotion I'd ever heard or seen from him—and I'd placed Sisu into his arms just moments after his birth. The guardian's only child.

"So is Drake." Suanmi tapped her long fingernails on the arm of her chair. They were filed into slightly rounded points, painted bright red. "Yet he is perfectly capable."

Drake was Suanmi's ward and the far seer's apprentice, but I'd only seen him in passing at various gatherings.

"Capable of utterly wanton destruction," Haoxin said gleefully. As if wanton destruction was a good thing.

"Dusk." Suanmi leaned forward slightly, drawing my attention firmly to her. "We are creating a position for you, under the purview of...the guardians and no others."

I frowned, briefly wondering what correction she'd paused to make. "I'm an archivist, guardian—"

"Yes, yes. A perfect guise. You were selected for this honor for a reason." She tilted her head thoughtfully, muttering to herself. In French, I thought, but without Infinity in hand, I couldn't translate it. "A perfect guise? Disguise?"

Haoxin groaned. I thought it sounded a little like, 'Kill me now.'

"A guise, guardian?" I prompted, concerned that the conversation was about to take another detour. I felt certain that we were nowhere near the point of why I'd been brought to the nexus. The bones of my face were starting to ache. I didn't know if the sensation was from stress or from the exposure to so much magic. From the room. I couldn't feel a drop of power from the guardians themselves.

So probably stress. Because as a dragon, I was actually all but immune to magic. Or at least any magic with malicious intent. Otherwise, I wouldn't be able to reap any of the multitude of magic's benefits.

My gaze flicked to Jiaotu. Again. Benefits such as the magical birth control that my mother hadn't bothered taking. Though then I wouldn't have Sisu, so—

"Yes," Suanmi said, smiling. The expression was disconcertingly wide, almost manically gleeful. "We require a … representative."

"A spy." Haoxin snorted. "Because you don't trust the others."

My heart started hammering in my chest, so hard that I knew the guardians had to be able to hear it. "Others?" I asked, squeaking unbecomingly.

"The Adept," Haoxin said mildly. "We would never ask you to report on your own." She cast a look at the older guardians. "Well, I wouldn't."

I nodded as if I had any idea what they were talking about. My heart rate did, however, settle slightly. For a moment, I had truly thought they wanted some sort of internal spy, and...

Wait.

"You want me to work...ah, to live among the Adept?" I blurted, interrupting the staring contest going on between Haoxin and Suanmi.

"Yes," Jiaotu said. "We will find you a position suited to your talents, and you will simply live among them. And be...available."

Available? "For what?" My mind was whirling. But I couldn't figure out if that meant I was thrilled or overwhelmed. Both, maybe. But the responsibility. The—

"Times are changing," Haoxin said.

"Times continually change," Pulou said, correcting her.

She ignored the elder dragon. "The Adept will not be able to remain hidden from the humans for much longer. Technology is advancing too quickly. And magic is...shifting, if not fading from the world."

That wasn't a new idea. Not exactly. Many of the Adept felt that magic was waning under the oppressive influence of environmentally destructive technology. I had no concrete data to back up that supposition, but the theory felt sound to me. I just had no idea that the guardian dragons would concern themselves with such mundane possibilities. Most of the Adept didn't even know that guardians existed outside of morality tales.

A jot of some emotion shot through my chest. Fear maybe, but most likely anxiety. I'd never realized how sheltered I'd been from basic emotions until the last few minutes. I really wasn't dealing with the sudden onslaught well. Perhaps it was easy to be tranquil and focused when...not losing hold of your brother while crossing into a pocket dimension that you had absolutely no control over, then getting embroiled into some guardian plot to … to … what?

That 'what' still wasn't clear to me.

"You want me … you want me to walk among them as a dragon?"

"No," Suanmi said.

"Well, not right away," Haoxin amended. "We place you among Adepts and humans. You will need to live among them to understand and absorb their concerns and whatnot. And maybe it comes to nothing."

I was nodding again, as if I understood. Which I still didn't. So I stopped nodding, and no doubt looked like an idiot.

"I'll … I'll need a last name," I stammered, having no idea why that was my primary issue with their proposal. Their … assignment.

A mission?

They wanted to recruit a twenty-five-year-old archivist who had stepped into the human world no more than three times a year throughout her entire life. To live and work among the Adept. I would need an entire identity. A house, money. I didn't even know where they wanted to send me. And Sisu …

"Use Zhi." Suanmi crossed her legs, brushing nonexistent lint off her knee. The soles of her spiked heels were bright red, matching her nail polish.

I felt like a grubby street urchin standing before her. Actually, I wasn't certain street urchins were a regular thing anymore. I hadn't noted any running around London the few times I'd visited. But the English literature section of the estate library hadn't been updated in at least a hundred years, and I had a difficult time ordering fiction from the bookstores I had access to that wasn't just as ancient.

I waited, awkwardly caught in the moment, for one of the other guardians to interject. To correct the fire breather. Though 'Zhi' was the overall name for the branch of the archivists I was descended from, it wasn't appropriate for me to take as a surname among the Adept. I wasn't Chinese. I didn't even specialize in Asian culture.

No one spoke.

I flushed, clearing my throat. "I don't look Chinese. Or even Asian."

As one, five of the most powerful beings in the world homed in on me. Then blinked.

"It would be a flagrant appropriation ..."

Suanmi huffed, clearly peeved. "What about... Book? That's English. They still take their surnames from their occupations, don't they?"

"How is 'book' an occupation?" Haoxin sneered.

"Booker," the fire breather snapped, displeased.

"You ..." I twined my fingers together, then forced myself to release them and relax my shoulders. Be professional. "You want me to disguise myself as an archivist named ... Booker? And I'm not to be ... a dragon?"

"Oh for gods' sake!" Haoxin snarled. "Just make her a Godfrey! She can pass for a witch ..." She waved her hand in the guardian of Northern Europe's direction. "Jiaotu can glamour her. And then, with the Godfrey connection, there will be someone powerful on hand to clean up her messes."

Messes?

I didn't make messes.

The power going out across a couple of blocks after Infinity absorbed the tablet and its connection to the Wi-Fi could have been a complete coincidence.

Okay.

I didn't *usually* make messes.

"A glamour to conceal her power won't hold," Jiaotu said, "if Dusk uses too much magic."

Suanmi sniffed. "If you aren't up to the task, guardian, then—"

Energy shifted through the vast chamber, rising to stir around my ankles. I waited, heart thumping—again—to see which one of the guardians was going to spring forth and—

Their collective gaze shifted to my feet. Multiple eyebrows rose. Suanmi and Jiaotu grimaced. A slow grin curled Haoxin's lips.

I looked down. A short branch speckled with light-pink blossoms had settled against my booted toe, its petals still stirring as if in a fading breeze. I reached down and plucked it up.

The air was scented with honey and a touch of … citrus.

The branch had been cleanly cut, the flowers fully formed, stamens still tipped with puffs of yellow pollen. From a cherry tree, I thought, but I wasn't an expert in botany.

Suanmi murmured something in Cantonese that I didn't catch, speaking to Jiaotu. He shook his head slightly, regarding me with narrowed eyes.

"That's settled, then." Haoxin smiled smugly. "Dusk Zhi Godfrey. I'll put you in touch with Pearl Godfrey, who also heads the witches Convocation. She can help facilitate …" She flicked her hand offishly. "… everything."

My entire life was about to be packed into that 'everything.'

"With her backing," Haoxin continued, "none of the witches will question your Godfrey credentials. You could be a long-lost niece or a cousin or whatever suits."

"It might have simply been a brownie," Suanmi said, glaring at the branch of blossoms I held at my side.

It wasn't. It was the aspect of my archivist's power again, still not fully understood. But I knew that it often manifested as an encouragement. An urging for me to take the next step. Or perhaps a confirmation that I was traversing the correct path.

"A brownie? Violating the sacred space of the chamber?" Haoxin said snottily. "No. You felt what I felt."

Suanmi sniffed, settling back in her throne. "Fine."

"My son, my family, will not be known as God-freys!" Jiaotu sneered.

Suanmi eyed him.

Haoxin leaned forward, grinning with anticipation, as if she expected a fight to break out and didn't want to miss a moment of it.

Tension ran through the guardian of Northern Europe's jaw as he held the gaze of the fire breather, but he didn't offer any other protest. Not out loud, anyway. It was possible that the guardians could choose to communicate telepathically, even though the far seer wasn't presently with them.

As a junior archivist, I wasn't privy to that level of information. I also had no idea if Jiaotu was protesting his son taking on any witch identity or specifically the Godfrey name. If it was the Godfrey coven he loathed, I didn't know the reason or the connection. As far as I knew, the Godfrey witches didn't have any significant presence within his territory.

Suanmi turned her dispassionate gaze on me, dismissing Jiaotu.

I avoided dropping my own eyes. I wasn't required to do so with the guardians, but most dragons revered the nine. And it wasn't as if, on the whole, I didn't feel the same. But I wasn't entirely certain I trusted their…judgement.

It was my future being discussed. Mine and Sisu's.

"London and the British Museum is the obvious choice," Suanmi said. "The collection is vast on both the human and the Adept side. Dusk would have no trouble hiding in plain sight, and…" She tapped her blood red fingernails on the arm of her throne. "Occupying herself."

I really shouldn't have been internally blistering at everything that came out of the fire breather's mouth. It wasn't remotely professional of me, nor did she mean everything she was saying.

Okay, she meant it. But it was from her perspective, her position of power. She wasn't intentionally insulting me. Still, I struggled to keep my expression neutral.

"London?" Haoxin scoffed. "Planning on forcing Dusk to clean up your vampire problem?"

Me cleaning up a vampire problem? That sounded like a terrible idea. Not only wasn't I that sort of dragon, but I had Sisu to protect. Just because dragon blood was poison to vampires—and to demons for that matter—didn't mean they wouldn't try to snatch a five-year-old fledgling. To ransom. Or simply just to prove that they could. Most Adepts collected power in any of its many forms, but vampires even more so—likely because they were ostracized by other magic users. Though I had no doubt there were exceptions to that well-documented rule.

"Problem?" Suanmi smirked. "He amuses me. That is all."

"So we're in agreement then," Haoxin said. "No to London."

The fire breather shrugged. "I do understand that he has a large collection of his own. Perhaps he'd be open to having Dusk curate it."

Jiaotu stiffened. "Sisu is my son. Dusk is his current guardian. That vampire that so amuses you is thousands of years old. His shiver is the largest in the world."

Suanmi shrugged. "Bring Sisu here, then. If you're concerned that Dusk can't protect him. Train him with Drake."

I almost opened my mouth at that dig, except it wasn't actually directed at me.

"He's five," Jiaotu snapped. "His mother is already…wandering. I won't have him separated from his sister."

Suanmi curled her lip. "He'll have to leave her at some point."

"Not today." The white-blond guardian of Northern Europe tapped his fingers on the arm of his chair, lifting his chin as he spoke. "Oslo."

"That collection isn't large enough for the talent of one such as Dusk," the fire breather said. "Her guise would be shredded on the first day. And Oslo is too isolated. Too few Adepts for Dusk to learn anything, or to be able to oversee effective…change, should it become necessary."

'Effective change' sounded like something completely outside of my abilities—especially with a pause in between the words. That was something a sword-wielding, armor-wearing dragon would be much better at—

"Compromise," Suanmi purred. "Berlin."

"Boston," Haoxin interjected before Jiaotu could offer a counter.

"You have the Godfreys," Pulou said, interjecting himself into the main conversation for the first time.

"On the West Coast," Haoxin protested. "And what's the point of naming Dusk a Godfrey if we don't place her in North America?"

"She will pass easier in Europe," Suanmi declared.

"Agreed." The treasure keeper narrowed his eyes at me, as if in assessment. "A head curator position in Dublin was recently vacated. I'd prefer London myself. I'm quite certain the Dunkirk witches are hoarding that which they shouldn't. But if we ousted one of their own, or created a new position for Dusk, they'd be suspicious. And suspicious witches can be annoyingly persistent."

"Oh, yes!" Bixi perked up suddenly. And literally. She sat ramrod straight with her hands on her knees, dark eyes suddenly drilling into my soul. "Dublin! There was that incident...with the Egyptian mummy that wasn't actually a pharaoh."

She paused, tipping her head just enough to let me know I was to continue the tale, to illuminate the others.

"Yes," I said. "A soul sucker of some sort. Several witches went missing, including the head curator. My Great-Uncle Jamal was called in, and he vanquished the being back into its sarcophagus. But...ah...he had to vacate his position."

I flicked my gaze to Jiaotu. His expression was cool, lounging back with a hand flung over his crossed knees. So I continued. "My mother took over for Uncle Jamal as the head of the Egyptian archives in Giza, guardian. Six years ago."

Referring to the timeline was a dig, and utterly unprofessional of me when dealing with elder beings. But the so-called 'incident' in Dublin had left my great-uncle—who was over three hundred years old and an exceedingly skilled archivist—thinking he was a mummy for over seven months, even though he'd defeated the soul sucker.

We'd actually had to feed my Great-Uncle Jamal intravenously, and he had to relearn how to speak English. Actually, how to speak, read, and write any language other than the ancient Egyptian he still defaulted to even six years later.

The missing witches hadn't fared as well. Though I was surprised the head curator position was still open.

It was Jamal who was currently traveling with Mom. For eleven months now. More than once since they'd left, I had wondered whether taking my great-uncle with her, as opposed to someone more…reliable had been the wrong choice on my mother's part.

"Ah, yes," Bixi said, clapping her hands together. "I remember. Jamal is of my blood. I kept the nasty entity. It is most decorative now."

Pulou frowned. "You kept the soul sucker? And have it housed in …?" He flicked his gaze to me, then back at the elder guardian, changing tack. "It would be my privilege, Bixi, She of All Forms—"

Bixi sighed. "Yes, yes, treasure keeper. See me in my chambers. You can have it."

"I have no issue with Dublin," Suanmi said, smiling thinly. All of Ireland was in the fire breather's territory. She raised an eyebrow at Jiaotu, as if daring him to retort.

He simply smiled as he spoke. "I claimed Trissa and Dusk at the birth of my son. I walk freely wherever they reside."

Suanmi's eyes narrowed.

Mine widened. Because that was a surprise—Jiaotu's claiming of me, meaning I was under his protection even if I left his territory. I'd had no idea.

"If Dusk is situated in Ireland," Suanmi said coolly, "she will report to me. That supersedes your claim."

Jiaotu straightened, gazing down at me. "What say you, Dusk Zhi Godfrey, sister of my firstborn son, daughter of my mate, Trissa?" Magic boomed through the chamber, accentuating each of his words. "Do you accept my offer of protection? Will you consent to being my vassal? My eyes and ears in the modern world?"

My brain…stuttered. And for a moment, I didn't know what to say, how to respond. It was obvious that there was more going on than simply moving me into the head curator position in Dublin to keep tabs on the Adept.

"Dusk." Jiaotu's power twined around me, waiting for my acceptance. "For your brother."

I nodded. The energy riding his words settled over my shoulders, then dissipated as if it had simply re-inforced a bond that had already been in place. A bond I'd been previously unaware of.

"Fine," Suanmi said. She didn't sound at all ruffled. In fact, she sounded a little bit pleased. "Feel free to visit Sisu and Dusk in Ireland." The fire breather flicked her amused gaze to me. "As will I."

Apparently, even guardian dragons played games with each other.

I swallowed, gripping the branch of cherry blossoms in my right hand as I nodded. Again. Though I still wasn't completely clear what exactly was being asked of me.

There really wasn't anything else I could do but say yes—but there was absolutely no way I was even tempted to say no. An official position? Under the directive of the guardians? At twenty-five?

Zeke and my mother were going to lose their minds.

A conversation in rapid-fire Cantonese exploded among four of the guardians. Bixi rose, not part of it, crossing toward me on bare feet. All her golden chains were tinkling against each other. She stretched her hand out as if to cup my chin, but didn't actually touch me. I met her dark-eyed gaze obligingly. She stared at me intently. Her expression was almost blank, as if she wasn't actually looking at me. As if she was perhaps looking beyond me, deep into the generations she'd already crossed through herself.

Jiaotu shifted, so that he was leaning on the opposite arm of his chair. Still bickering lazily with the others, but seemingly also keeping an eye on me. Or, more specifically, on Bixi.

"I see," the guardian of Northern Africa murmured. "You have secrets barely hidden skin deep, Dusk Zhi Godfrey. He will not be able to keep them contained for much longer."

I had no idea what she was talking about. Though I could feel the claim that the simple utterance of my full new name placed on me.

The casual power of a guardian.

Apparently, Bixi had been paying attention to at least some of the conversation.

"I shall also be exerting my right as a grandmother," Bixi said. "If only to check on your mother. Eleven months. I was wondering why I missed her."

Unsure of how to address the elder guardian, I stumbled over my reply. "It would be an honor to have you—"

She flicked her fingers dismissively, then wandered off without looking at or addressing anyone else. She simply disappeared into the vastness of the chamber. No door or portal opened.

Regardless of whatever the others were discussing in Cantonese, whatever issue had demanded a quorum was apparently resolved. I hadn't heard the guardians vote, but perhaps they didn't operate as a democracy in that specific way. Perhaps my acceptance of Jiaotu's claim had been enough. By nodding, I had agreed to...

I rapidly pieced together the jumble of conversation I'd just partially participated in, disregarding all the sniping and the games being played. I still had no idea why I'd been called to the chamber in the first place, because it wasn't as if I'd had any say in anything that had been discussed. In anything that had been decided for me. And for Sisu.

I'd been tasked to walk among the Adept as the guardians' representative. And to fill the position as the head curator of the Dublin collection of magical antiquities, which I recalled was housed in a section of the National Museum of Ireland. That was clear.

It was a dream job, though not a position traditionally filled by a dragon archivist. Hence the strange caveats—namely, that I had to pretend to be a Godfrey witch, to spy on my coworkers, and to oversee 'effective change' should it be needed.

Which meant what exactly?

Helping transition the Adept, and the guardians specifically, into the twenty-first century? If so, they were two-plus decades late.

I was woefully ill prepared. For all three tasks—the position, the spying, and the so-called effective change.

Of course, there was always the possibility that the guardians placed me in Dublin, then completely forgot I was there or that I was tasked with any sort of mission.

Best-case scenario.

And a completely plausible outcome.

If Jiaotu hadn't been watching me so closely, I might have been able to slip from the chamber without any of them noticing. The argument was simmering down to only Haoxin and Suanmi now, with Pulou fiddling with some magical device he'd pulled out of his fur coat pocket. Except there didn't appear to be a door leading out of the chamber. Or an easily accessible passageway.

And wandering after Bixi seemed like a dreadful idea.

Plus, I was still a little confused about the idea of being presented as a Godfrey witch. Disguised. Posing as a long-lost niece or grandchild?

I didn't even know what branch of witch magic the Godfreys wielded. Or whether or not I was capable of faking it.

I was magic. All dragons were capable of casting and whatnot. But whether or not those spells or intents actually ignited was a completely different matter. It was easy to overpower such things. And dragons weren't especially delicate, not even archivists and...

The remaining guardians were staring at me. It was possible they had been for some time. A quiet had settled over the chamber. It wasn't uncomfortable, but it did have an actual weight.

"It's settled then," Suanmi pronounced in English. She cast a sidelong look at Jiaotu.

He grimaced. "I have property in Dublin."

"Yes," Suanmi purred. "I know you do."

I was most definitely being caught up within some sort of guardian manipulation. Some part of this discussion, this transaction, had nothing to do with me—the lowly archivist—and everything to do with Suanmi gaining power over Jiaotu. Or perhaps the other way around.

"You'll sign the property over to Dusk," Haoxin said. "In its entirety."

Both guardians of Europe swiveled to look at the guardian of North America, visibly aghast.

She smiled at them prettily, then settled her keen-eyed gaze on me. I wasn't the only one aware of the games being played. Though it was unlikely that the youngest guardian was as in the dark as I was.

"I've already made Dusk my vassal." Jiaotu waved his hand dismissively. "She is fully protected—"

"No," the petite blond interrupted. "You're asking Dusk to upend her life. To shorten her apprenticeship by three-quarters of a century, while still taking care of your son. You will deed the property to her, under the name Dusk Zhi Godfrey. Free and clear, with enough funds to manage the estate for at least a hundred years."

"Money ..." Suanmi sneered.

"You want her to live among the Adept, don't you?" Haoxin pressed.

Jiaotu opened his mouth to protest.

Suanmi and Haoxin looked at him expectantly.

His nostrils flared. "Yes. Of course."

Suanmi smiled.

I noted the fire breather's smug reaction at the same time Haoxin did. The blond guardian narrowed her eyes. I had the distinct impression that all of us were somehow being directed by Suanmi—me and the other guardians alike. But to what end, I had no idea.

I might never know. For all their posturing and the threats of visiting, it seemed likely that I might never see any of the guardians again. Other than Jiaotu when he came to visit Sisu.

"I reserve the right to visit Dusk as I will," Pulou said, his tone casual.

Ah. So maybe I was wrong.

Suanmi's shoulders stiffened.

"She is, after all, my archivist."

"That is debatable, treasure keeper," the fire breather said. "The archivists oversee all our individual history, not simply the main archives that are under your care. Placing Dusk in Dublin—"

"Which has a mixed collection," the treasure keeper interjected, his tone still even and sure—though he was obviously inserting himself into whatever game was still being played. "From all eras. If you'd wanted Dusk as your personal archivist, she didn't need a change in title. The modern world was already her specialty."

Suanmi straightened imperiously. "I am older than you!"

"When Dusk requires the attention of a guardian, she will communicate with me," Jiaotu interjected.

"Yes, yes," Pulou said dismissively. "We all watched you puff out your chest and claim the archivist."

"I...did...no such thing!"

Haoxin started laughing quietly.

If I concentrated hard enough, I wondered if I could tap into the dimensional space in which the chamber was situated. Perhaps I could open the doorway back to the nexus. Or to Jiaotu's rooms to retrieve Sisu. Time passed differently from pocket to pocket, but my brother had to be missing me by now.

Though...the nexus library was extensive, and very few archivists gained access to it. I could suggest that I needed to gather more information, specific to the Dublin collection, in order to prepare for my new position...

Oh, yes.

My new position.

I was going to be heading a department of magical antiquities.

I had no idea how to do that.

I mean, my sensory abilities were well honed. A rare talent, in fact. And, of course, I knew how to curate and catalogue and...

The guardians were staring at me.

Again.

No. They were staring at the door that had appeared on my left, hovering a few centimeters from the ground and seemingly suspended by nothing.

"Going somewhere?" Haoxin asked, amused.

"Oh!" I swallowed. "Was that...me?"

Suanmi sighed. Heavily.

Pulou chuckled. "You were thinking of somewhere you needed to be within the nexus?"

"The library," I said. Then I firmed my tone. "The position you'd like me to undertake requires a slightly different knowledge base. A shift from my more-modern focus. My mother's library is out of date on most knowledge areas outside of Egyptian, Greek, and—"

Pulou waved his hand, smirking. "Go. The library is obviously willing to open for you. Your elders will sort out the other...details."

I glanced at the plain wooden door hanging suspended beside me. It didn't appear to lead anywhere. As in, I could have walked around it unimpeded.

I might have been only twenty-five, but even I knew that I shouldn't walk through doors simply because they presented themselves.

"She's not going alone," Haoxin snapped. "Why am I the voice of reason around here today?"

"Because you still remember what it's like to be mortal," Pulou said. Then he waved his hand toward the door. "Wait at the entrance, archivist. I'll find you an escort that the library will have a difficult time beguiling."

The door clicked, then swung open. If I looked at it straight on, a marbled antechamber stood on the other side. If I angled my head, nothing appeared behind the door.

"May I have permission to bring Infin...my personal archive with me?" I asked. I had almost named Infinity in front of guardians. They'd think I was an idiot.

The scarred wooden table appeared in the center of the antechamber beyond the door. It held my backpack, my daggers, and Infinity.

"The library can be a little...finicky," Haoxin said. "About foreign magic."

"She's an archivist." Suanmi sighed, exasperated. "Her ancestors' power built the library in the first place."

That was news to me. My right palm instantly started itching. Despite having an exceptional memory, I desperately loved the scratch of a pen on paper, and feeding ink and words and knowledge onto the page. I felt that real physical reaction whenever I acquired something needing documentation. Plus writing things down cemented them in my mind.

"Don't leave the nexus without speaking to me, Dusk," Jiaotu said.

"Yes, guardian."

"He'll need your signature," Haoxin said smugly.

Jiaotu cast a withering look at the youngest guardian. She ignored him, still smiling.

I met the guardian of Northern Europe's blue-eyed gaze. The same blue eyes that most often twinkled with mischief on my brother's face were cool and reserved on the guardian. "Sisu?" I said.

He nodded. "I'll have him join you."

I cast a quick gaze across the four remaining guardians, then bowed awkwardly. "Thank you for the honor, guardians."

Haoxin snorted.

Suanmi sighed. Again.

"Don't enter the library unaccompanied, Dusk," Pulou said once more. Then he grunted as if just remembering something. From a pocket of his fur coat, he pulled a thick, dark-brown leather-bound book, holding it out to me. "You'll want this. A gift from my personal collection. The library will not yield any books to you."

Suanmi tilted her head, reading the gilded title etched across the front cover. She smirked, highly amused.

I stepped forward, grasping the spine of the tome, bowing slightly to accept the gift. The book thrummed with magic.

Witch magic.

"A gift," Pulou repeated to my bowed head. "Otherwise the library might try to keep it. And you."

Energy passed between Pulou and me. I inhaled sharply, but the power settled quickly across the back of my hand. Pulou released the book. It was heavier than it looked.

Barely stopping myself from petting the tome while cooing terms of endearment to it, I glanced at the title. *Useful Spells, Basic Brews, and Other Fundamental Conjuring.* It was a grimoire. "Oh, thank you, guardian."

"It should be of some help," he said dryly. "And, since you're to masquerade as a Godfrey, I'd pay attention to the sections on charm and charisma."

Suanmi snorted derisively.

"You only wish he was joking," Haoxin said.

It was becoming more than obvious that the God-frey witches were held in vastly different regard by the guardians. I, of course, had no idea why. And my ignorance was becoming an irksome theme.

"You are dismissed," Suanmi said coolly. Her gaze was fixed to Haoxin, not me.

I told myself I was imagining the licks of fire in her hazel eyes. But I also quickly averted my gaze just in case I was mistaken.

It might have been difficult to kill a dragon, but the fire breather could murder me with a single breath.

"Thank you," I murmured again, crossing to and stepping through the doorway into the marbled antechamber. The door shut behind me, completely disappearing.

I was alone. With only a basic understanding of what I'd just agreed to do for the guardian nine.

Saying 'no' to them might not have been an option. But having said 'yes,' I wasn't going to give the guardians any reason to regret selecting me for the task. No matter how daunting the prospect was, I was going to be the head curator of a significant magical archive. That was…thrilling.

And a solid to-do list was certain to ease some of the confusion and uncertainty. It always did. I particularly enjoyed crossing items off.

CHAPTER THREE

HALLWAYS BRANCHED FROM THE ANTECHAMBER IN three directions, including one that I'd seen through the doorway. A fourth columned archway opened up to a library. A mind-boggling, senses-overwhelming library. I stumbled, catching myself on the edge of the weathered wooden table as I tried to process the immensity of the collection that stood ahead of me.

Without tearing my gaze away from the shelves stretching impossibly high—all haphazardly piled with books and the occasional artifact—I settled my hand on Infinity.

My archive hummed gently under my touch.

Its energy was still unusually quiet, even deeply sleepy. But Infinity was definitely awake, once again aware.

Relief flooded through me. My knees actually weakened under the onslaught, under the emotional release of everything I'd been holding at bay since Infinity had gone inert, since losing Sisu. And from standing before the guardians without faltering.

I gently ran my fingers along the spine of the archive. The bronzed leather cover puckered, then split, revealing a golden eye with a narrow black pupil. The eye blinked slowly, then disappeared.

Well, that was new.

I laughed, confused but utterly delighted.

Then Infinity's energy withdrew further, as if the archive had responded to my touch to reassure me but was still in the process of recovering from its connection to the Internet.

My stomach soured. Again. I felt awful. Again. As if I'd done something wrong, as if I'd hurt Infinity. And the abrupt manifestation of an eye—possibly indicating that the archive was aware, even sentient—didn't help.

It was also possible that I was projecting my own emotional state onto my personal archive. Inanimate objects, magical or not, didn't have feelings.

The manifestation of the eye could be the result of the archive spending time in the nexus, surrounded by the sheer power that emanated from a magical construct set outside space and time. I made a mental note to check Great-Grandfather George's journals for any mention of his own archive and whether or not it had reacted this way.

I retrieved my daggers, sliding them into my forearm sheaths. Then I tucked the grimoire gifted to me by the treasure keeper into my backpack and pulled it over my shoulders. Sisu's pack was already gone.

I kept Infinity in my left hand, as usual.

The table disappeared.

"Thank you," I murmured under my breath, acknowledging the brownies still invisibly serving me—and silently marveling at their ability to keep nine guardians and their various apprentices and retainers in line. Brownies usually didn't like being acknowledged or praised for anything they saw as their vocation, but I preferred to be polite when possible.

I stepped closer to the archway that opened into the library, carefully marking where the marble flooring transitioned into polished hardwood and staying back a step. As instructed.

I might have totally wrangled the invitation to enter the nexus library, but I wasn't stupid. I had at least three direct ancestors who'd never returned from so-called incidents between the stacks that currently stretched before me. And they hadn't been twenty-five-year-old junior archivists at the time of their deaths or disappearances.

A burgundy-and-red handwoven rug was set just beyond the archway. Its dark-gold fringe practically teased the line of transition between white marble and oak. I wasn't well versed enough to make a definitive assessment simply by sight, but I thought the patterning might have been Persian, late fifteenth or early sixteenth century. It was an odd decorating choice, though, because it was too small for the space it was meant to cover.

Loosely stacked books with a variety of leather, paper, and fabric bindings were piled on the hardwood floor to either side of the archway. Crumpled pages and torn bindings abounded, as if these were piles of books that needed repair. I caught myself reaching for the nearest stack. Not to catalogue them—that would be rude—but just to straighten them, to tidy them. Fold the bent pages back and—

Infinity hummed, vibrating intensely against my inner wrist and lower ribcage.

I withdrew my hand.

The hum emanating from the archive faded, withdrawing into that sleepy state I'd noted earlier.

Had that been a warning? To not touch the damaged books?

If so, that was also new.

Each archivist built their own personal archive. It wasn't much talked about, because the process was so individual. Though I had read brief descriptions and accounts in the personal journals housed in the family library, archivists didn't touch each other's personal archives. No one touched Infinity, not even my mother. Not since the day she'd presented the archive to me—along with the title of Archivist of the Modern World that Suanmi had sneered at so thoroughly.

It was possible that tying Infinity to the Wi-Fi in the Oslo cafe had been … not a bad idea exactly, but definitely an interesting one. What with the eye appearing, and the feeling that Infinity was somehow trying to reassure me. And now the warning.

But there was no one I could ask. The Internet was so new that I was the only archivist to have been born during its inception and growth.

Wait …

Maybe my title and position wasn't just a way to keep me busy. Maybe an Archivist of the Modern World was important in this technologically dominated era. And that sudden understanding made the task I'd just been assigned by the guardians more … fitting. Though still completely overwhelming, of course. But if the centuries-old and epically powerful dragons needed an … emissary? Then a modern archivist, rather than a warrior dragon, would be the best choice.

Given that, it was possible that Infinity would adapt to me specifically—to my focus, my intent. I'd caught my mother having long conversations with her own archive—a large black-leather tome with smooth, gilded pages that was sometimes three times the size of Infinity and sometimes small enough to be tucked into a pocket. Those overheard chats hadn't sounded one-sided, though I'd only ever heard my mother speaking. As far as I knew, she hadn't even named her archive.

I read to Infinity. I fed the archive information as I wrote on the thick pages that eagerly soaked up my favorite ink—a deep brown, speckled with 24-carat gold. But Infinity didn't talk back. Not yet.

Not with words, at least.

A delighted shriek echoed through from one of the other corridors behind me, reverberating around the antechamber.

Sisu.

I turned, already grinning, to catch sight of Jiaotu striding through the far archway with my brother on his shoulders.

My smile faltered at the sight of the guardian of Northern Europe. He almost appeared to smile back at me and then ... didn't.

"Dusk!" Sisu crowed. He was brandishing a steel shortsword.

Guardians might have been practically immortal, but I personally wouldn't have given a five-year-old a sword and then walked around with him on my shoulders.

I inclined my head at the guardian in question.

He reciprocated.

But before I could greet him more formally, Sisu stood up on his shoulders and launched himself at me.

I dropped Infinity, reaching for my brother and catching him just under his armpits. His momentum forced me backward. Stumbling, we listed sideways. Sisu's blade whooshed by my ear to settle on my shoulder, flat side down. I set him on the ground. He was chortling so madly he didn't seem to have control of his legs, so I held him upright.

We were standing within the library.

Our feet were on the hardwood, though. Not on the fringed rug.

I would have sworn that the rug had been closer to the transition point between the rooms.

Sisu stopped laughing, abruptly making a break for the nearest pile of books. I grabbed for him, managing to snag a fistful of his backpack and holding him back. His fingers—and sword—were stretched toward what appeared to be a golden egg propped up on an open book I hadn't noticed before. The book was filled with neat, black-inked handwriting that covered pages and pages of thin vellum. A seam ran through the widest part of the egg, as if it unscrewed. Or perhaps it was hinged.

Either way, it was never, ever a good idea to touch or collect a golden egg. Eggs had only one purpose. To hatch.

In this case, the egg held something undoubtedly magical—and far too powerful to be housed anywhere but in the guardian nexus.

"Careful with the sword, please," I said evenly. "You'd be upset if you damaged anything."

Still hanging forward against my hold, Sisu glanced over his shoulder at me. Then he brandished his new sword, grinning widely. The blade was perfectly sized for him. Its steel was free of embellishments—and, without a doubt, magically sharpened. Dragons didn't believe in practice weapons.

Sisu got his feet under him, but I kept hold of his backpack. His attention was still trained on the egg.

Jiaotu huffed quietly. It might have been a pleased laugh. He was still watching us from the antechamber. Thoughtfully, perhaps.

The guardian of Northern Europe, aka one of the nine most powerful beings in the world, scooped up

Infinity from where I'd dropped it, then strode toward us.

He passed the archive to me, touching it without any obvious ramifications. I'd tried brushing a fingertip against my mother's archive once. My skin had been singed for days after. But then, Jiaotu was a guardian after all.

"Never force your sister to choose between her archive and you," he said sternly, speaking to Sisu.

"Yes, guardian." My brother arranged his face into his best 'look how agreeable I am' expression.

Jiaotu shook his head, took the sword from Sisu, and somehow slid it into my brother's backpack. A sheath had apparently been built into the pack while I'd been chatting with the guardians.

Hours, if not days, had slipped by.

Jiaotu released the sword and it disappeared.

The sheath was spelled.

That was so going to be a problem later.

I touched Sisu's shoulder, worried about how long he'd been in the nexus without me, and possibly not knowing where I'd been. But his attention turned back to the golden egg as if it was somehow compelling him. And maybe it was. I couldn't feel any specific magic from the egg, but the press of the library's energy was intense.

Jiaotu reached over his son's head, plucking up the object of Sisu's obsession. He narrowed his bright-blue eyes at the artifact, which was only slightly larger than a regular chicken egg. Then he shrugged and handed it to Sisu.

An entire world of hurt and terror could have been hidden in that shrug.

Sisu cupped the egg in both hands, grinning. Then he whispered, "Hello there."

And … that was way worse than a casual shrug.

Jiaotu was watching me with one eyebrow slightly raised, as if he expected me to protest.

I could handle anything that came out of the damn egg. I held the guardian's gaze, silently letting him know that.

His mouth quirked, though he instantly smoothed the expression, casting his gaze into the library. "I haven't visited in some time. Shall we have tea?" He strode forward before I could answer. "Or do you prefer coffee?"

"I'd like to access the Celtic section, guardian," I said.

He waved his hand over his shoulder. "Yes, yes. The books you require will find you."

"The books will..." A thrill unfurled in my belly, and I couldn't help the wide grin that swamped my face. I probably looked exactly like Sisu with his egg.

A shout sounded behind me, instantly muffled. I spun back just in time to see the fringed rug envelop my brother, rising to float above the floor. Sisu was still clutching the damn egg. Instead of rescuing himself.

In a blink, Jiaotu was moving past me. Twin axes had appeared in his hands, one raised to strike.

"No!" I cried before I could stop myself. "You'll ruin the rug."

Jiaotu paused midstrike, looking back at me, utterly incredulous. "You prefer it smother your brother?"

I raised my chin, ignoring the way my heart hammered in my chest over the fact that I'd just shouted at a demigod. "He is the child of a guardian, guardian. He doesn't smother easily. The rug, however, is likely irreplaceable."

"I would argue that your brother is the rarer object."

"Thankfully, you don't have to choose." My tone was stiff. A tiny voice in the back of my mind screamed that my lack of deference was going to get me reprimanded. Or worse.

Jiaotu lowered his axes, sweeping one forward to mockingly invite me to address the roiling rug and the muffled sounds emanating from within it.

Sisu sounded pissed, not panicked.

As I'd suspected when I'd seen its deliberate placement at the entrance, the rug was playful, not murderous. Which was why it had moved aside when we'd stumbled over the threshold. It couldn't grab both Sisu and me. And it wasn't stupid enough to try to grab a guardian.

Which, of course, was why Jiaotu was escorting us through the library in the first place.

Holding Infinity cradled in my left arm, I reached for the rolled rug. With Sisu still kicking within its confines, it lowered itself to match my height, its bottom edge hovering a few centimeters from the hardwood floor. I considered the design of the rug, but I still didn't know enough of the time period to assess the magical artifact visually. So instead, I followed my instincts.

The rug was either protecting the egg, protecting Sisu from the egg, or playing. Since there hadn't been enough time for the rug to form any sort of magical attachment to Sisu, and since the egg didn't have any markings that suggested it came from the same era as the rug, I settled on playful.

I experimentally ran my fingers through its wide fringe.

It tickled me in response.

Smiling, I started at the top of the rug and ran my fingers along one entire fringed edge, leaving a gentle kiss of my own power in the wake of my touch.

That fringed edge danced against my fingers and palm in return, tickling me back.

As with any object of power that I touched, I instantly picked up little details about the rug. It had been woven in 1327 by a powerful magic user as a gift for her...coven leader? That was a little unclear. The rug recalled being bloodied more than once in battle, and it had thwarted at least three attempts to bind it and steal it from its rightful owner. That owner was now dead.

I'd been completely wrong about the era.

I withdrew my hand before I got too caught up in accessing the history of the rug. An epic chronicle could have been written on it—as was often the way with magical objects deemed so powerful that they needed to be housed within the guardian nexus.

The rug unfolded, flattening to hover around waist height as it did. It revealed Sisu sitting at its center and still cupping the golden egg in both hands.

My brother grinned at me. "Hi!"

"Stay close to me or...your father, okay?"

Sisu blinked at Jiaotu thoughtfully. The guardian's expression was slightly bemused. Or possibly bored.

My brother presented the egg to me. I took it. The rug rotated without prompting, lowering itself so that I could tuck the golden egg into the outer pocket of Sisu's backpack.

I knew that if I were smart, I'd leave the egg behind when we left the library.

I just wasn't prepared to bear the onslaught of despair that Sisu would level at me for that betrayal. Also, it was one thing to bark orders at a guardian in the heat of the moment—watching the rug be destroyed would have been heartbreaking. But it was completely another thing to dare to curate the gifts he gave to his son.

That was most definitely shaky ground.

I zipped up the pack, stepping back.

"Thank you, archivist," Sisu said with utter sincerity. Then he patted the still-hovering rug and said, "Onward, my steed!"

The rug dumped him onto the hardwood floor, fluttering away almost huffily to settle again by the entrance.

"What did I do?" Sisu cried.

"What do you think?"

He glanced over at the rug, which appeared completely inanimate again. Then he grimaced. "I treated it like it belonged to me, not like a friend."

An oversimplification, but... "Yes."

"Tea?" Jiaotu said. His tone had taken on an edge of suffering.

Sisu scampered to his feet, practically flinging himself at his father. Jiaotu offered his hand to Sisu, and my brother took it. The resemblance between them was striking.

I didn't much look like either of my parents. At least not like the hazy memory I had of meeting my father once when I was very young. But when tanned, I was the spitting image of my maternal grandfather, Farhad. So much so that the few baby pictures of him in the family album always made me look twice.

Jiaotu led us to a reading nook that overlooked a lower level of the library. He settled into a high-backed brown leather chair in the corner by a carved wooden railing. Oversized and rough hewn, neither the chair, the railing, or the side table tucked to the guardian's left matched the almost-gaudy decor on display in most of the nexus.

The guardian crossed his legs, plucking a book from the top of a short stack set on the table. Seemingly undirected by anyone, a large wooden table and two matching chairs drifted in to fill the niche, answering my unvoiced question about the disparity in decor. The library—or, rather, the brownies in the library—were in charge, and had selected features that suited the guardian. The table was large enough for two.

Sisu climbed onto the nearest chair, removing his backpack.

Books began shifting and floating around the table, settling on the corners in what appeared to be two distinct piles.

The next book on the stack beside Jiaotu rose into the air. Not looking up from the book he was reading, the guardian settled his fingers on it, and it drifted back down.

I crossed to the far end of the table, already noting the Celtic-inspired designs on the covers of some of the books being magically sorted and reshuffled on that corner.

The corner next to Sisu was filling with what appeared to be children's books about mythology, ranging widely in era and origin. I brushed my fingers across the red, white, and black hardcover of one of those books as it slipped past me—a First Nations design, I thought—only to have it tugged just out of my reach.

As if I was being naughty by trying to touch what hadn't been offered to me.

Jiaotu smirked, though he was still reading the book propped open on his knee. "We all contribute to the library, including newer literature," he said without looking up. "But the collection has subsumed its current archivist."

I nodded. "My maternal great-grandfather George. Mom missed this year's attempt to extricate him."

"I suppose she must have." Jiaotu grimaced, flicking his gaze to Sisu. "I was unaware she'd been gone quite so long ... "

I followed his gaze, setting Infinity down on the table and slinging my backpack over the corner of my chair.

Sisu had changed his mind about sitting on his own chair, and was currently crouching a few steps away, digging through his pack. He unearthed what appeared to be a partially eaten peanut butter and raspberry jam sandwich wrapped in one of the beeswax wraps that brownies crafted. It confirmed that Sisu had been separated from me long enough that he'd needed to be fed at least one meal. Though I hadn't checked my backpack for it, I was fairly certain the sweet bun from the bakery was long gone.

He offered the sandwich to a nearby rug, but the rug wasn't intrigued. It was possible it was no more than it appeared to be—a long runner of fabric woven to protect the hardwood flooring between bookshelves.

"We're fine," I said to Jiaotu, chafing at the guardian's concern over our mother's absence.

"I know." His English was generally unaccented to my ear, though I wasn't certain what that said about my own accent. But when he got testy, his vowels lengthened.

So pretty much during any conversation in which I participated.

My backpack suddenly lifted from the chair of its own accord, hovering. The zippers opened, as if someone invisible was rifling through its contents. The broken tablet and numerous writing instruments were pulled from its depths. The grimoire from the treasure keeper started to briskly float away.

"I didn't give you permission to go through my things," I said mildly.

My backpack stilled. The contents, including the grimoire, were returned to it—with a reluctance I could practically feel. Then the pack settled on the corner of the chair again.

I sat down, carefully keeping a hand on Infinity.

Jiaotu was watching me with sharp blue eyes. The same shade as my brother's, yet they held nothing of Sisu's spirit.

I reached for the nearest stack of books. But before I could select one, a book bound in dark-green fabric lifted from the pile and settled into my grasp. Apparently, the library was going to control my reading order as well.

And that was just fine by me.

Who was I to question an archive that vast and powerful? Beyond protecting my personal property, of course.

"That tablet won't have survived crossing through the portal," Jiaotu said, flipping a page in his book.

"It broke before that," Sisu said, abandoning the inert rug in favor of stuffing the remaining sandwich in his mouth while climbing into the chair beside me.

"Oh?" Jiaotu said. "Why is your sister carrying around a broken piece of technology?"

Sisu knelt, clasping his hands together on the table and tilting his head thoughtfully while he chewed.

His father waited, one eyebrow raised.

Sisu swallowed. "I couldn't say."

Jiaotu hummed doubtfully. "Something to do with the incident at the coffee shop? In Oslo? That was where you were when we called for you, yes?"

Sisu laughed, completely delighted to be keeping a secret from his demigod father.

The guardian narrowed his eyes at his son. His expression was almost playful. "If it was serious, I would already know." He then flicked his gaze to me.

I quashed a smile. "Of course you would, guardian. It was beneath your notice. A glitch when magic met technology."

"And magic won."

It was a statement, not a question, but I placed my hand on Infinity and said, "I hope so."

Jiaotu smirked, then returned his attention to his book.

I was pleased to let the subject drop, happy to not sound like an inept idiot to a guardian who'd just tasked me with entering Adept society as his representative.

I opened Infinity toward the middle of the archive's pages, then opened the book the library had found for me—*Celtic Myths and other Magical Creatures*—at the beginning. I set the library book on top of Infinity, leaning over to eagerly scan the first page. It was written in English, but the phrasing pointed to the seventeenth or eighteenth century. The nexus library books didn't belong to me, couldn't belong to me, so I couldn't feed them into Infinity. It wasn't my place to collect them. But Infinity could absorb the information they held through physical contact.

My mother, along with the other archivists who were the head curators of their museums and magical archives, often liberated books from the nexus library. But only because they could make an argument that those books were better housed in more specific collections, and that the knowledge they provided should be more readily available.

I would have to catalogue the archives in Dublin to know if there were gaps in that collection, based on century and subject. And yes, the idea of doing so was as thrilling as it sounded.

Infinity's energy shifted in response to being offered the new book, but it felt sluggish. It was going to take time for my personal archive to absorb the text, possibly no faster than I could have read it. It was good to have the backup, though, even with my near perfect recall. I never wanted to worry about whether that inherent talent might fail me at exactly the wrong moment.

"Would you like some tea, then?" Jiaotu asked, seemingly put out for some reason.

My back stiffened. I hadn't asked to be babysat by him. "If you like, guardian."

He sighed heavily. "You'll have to request it."

I looked up questioningly.

The demigod closed and then tapped the book he was reading on his knee, grimacing. "I'm on the outs with the nexus brownies."

"What?" Sisu cried. "You upset Mistress Wintersprout?"

It most definitely took more than one brownie to oversee the nexus, but 'mistress' was the title held by the head brownie. Upset the mistress and, well…the guardian likely went hungry. A lot. And it was unlikely there were laundry facilities in the nexus, never mind a kitchen. Not one that the brownies would allow anyone else to access, at any rate.

Jiaotu laid a look on his son that rolled right off the aghast five-year-old. Sisu stood up in his chair, wagging his finger at his father. "What did you do?"

The guardian blinked, completely thrown.

My brother stamped his foot. "You should know better! You are the guardian of Northern Europe! The brownies only want to protect and serve you."

Jiaotu's expression blanked.

"Sisu," I whispered, worried that the demigod was about to lose his mind over being chided like a child. The fact that Sisu was simply echoing the argument we'd both heard from our estate's own brownies for many, many years was dreadfully amusing—but probably not to his guardian father.

"I brought in outside food," Jiaotu finally said.

Sisu huffed, placing his fisted hands on his hips, tapping his foot just like our own Mistress Brightshire did. But then he deflated slightly, glancing at me and whispering, "I don't know what outside food is."

Jiaotu chuckled quietly. "I was craving chicken souvlaki."

"Greek cuisine," I murmured to Sisu. "Remember when we had spanakopita and roasted potatoes?"

"Oh!" Sisu cried, climbing up on the table. The pile of books to his right came up to his waist. "And tzatziki with pita bread. Let's have that now."

"Tea will be fine," Jiaotu said, still clearly amused.

"I'll order." Sisu dramatically flung his arms out to the sides. "Please, may we have—"

An ornate silver tea service, replete with china cups and saucers, as well as a three-tiered tower of sandwiches and other treats, appeared at Sisu's feet. A traditional English tea, rather than Asian.

My brother crouched, reaching for one of the sandwiches.

"Off the table please," I said quietly.

He looked at me with sorrowful eyes. "But peanut butter and banana ..."

"Yes." Energy shifted through Infinity, indicating that it had absorbed the knowledge contained in the book quicker than I'd thought it would. I hadn't even managed to read the first paragraph. "And you may have a sandwich, and a cookie, once the tea is done steeping and you're seated properly."

Sisu grumbled, climbing down into his chair.

Disappointed, since I had actually wanted to read it for myself, I slid the library book to the side, reaching for the next one on the stack to my left. A brush of energy pressed a book bound in royal-blue fabric with a black leather spine into my hand. The cover was blank, no title or author name. The first book was whisked away toward the stacks.

I opened the new book on top of Infinity, noting with a great deal of satisfaction that it was handwritten. Possibly in Gaelic. A diary, perhaps? I scanned the opening pages, looking for numerals to give me an idea of the era.

Jiaotu unfolded himself from his chair, stepping up to the table. He served us tea with quick, efficient movements. Then he set half of a cucumber and cream cheese sandwich and two flower-shaped lemon cookies on a plate, sliding it across the table toward me. He served Sisu three tiny peanut butter and banana sandwiches, along with a strawberry macaroon.

"Thank you, Papa," Sisu murmured, tugging the china cup and saucer toward him to blow on his tea. It was mostly milk and sugar.

Jiaotu gently touched Sisu's bowed head, settling his gaze on me.

"Yes," I murmured, my attention on the book as the handwritten words ever so slowly resolved themselves into a rough English translation. Another of my innate talents, if I focused intently enough. "Thank you."

We read in silence. Jiaotu got up twice to retrieve Sisu from the stacks—though only after much squealing had occurred. I didn't wander off. As fast as I read or Infinity absorbed, the library kept feeding us books. Irish lore turned into Welsh, then Scottish.

I finished the last of the lemon cookies, and the tea service disappeared. The guardian across from me didn't complain about how much of his time I was wasting, or get called away, as he had every other time I'd spent more than a moment in his presence.

I looked up from the closing pages of a memoir written by a Welsh witch in the early 1900s to stretch my back and neck. My mind buzzed with input that would take me days to resolve into a cohesive recollection I could call forth when needed. Info that I somehow held in the back of my thoughts until the moment I had to recall it—another aspect of my personal magic. And anything I needed to clarify, or find other sources for, Infinity would provide. As long as I'd fed my archive the information, of course.

A thick roll of worn, light-brown leather appeared in the center of the table.

"Ah, finally," Jiaotu said, shifting forward in his chair. Sisu was perched on top of the nearest bookshelf, pretending to be a gargoyle looming over us. As his father stepped toward the table, Sisu launched himself off the shelf, shrieking.

Jiaotu caught him without even looking, setting him down on the table.

Despite the library's best efforts, children's books couldn't hold my brother's attention for hours. And I'd only managed to get him to nap for the time it took Infinity to absorb a single book—a collection of Scottish poems featuring beings of magic not often seen in the modern world. Beings long relegated to the status of creatures of myth among the nonmagicals.

Sisu hunkered down on the corner of the table with his gaze riveted to the leather roll, teeth bared and fingers spread to claws. Then he all but froze in place, still pretending he was a gargoyle. He'd had to break his persona in order to get a closer look at whatever the guardian of Northern Europe had been waiting for. Whatever he'd deemed worthy of being wrapped in antique leather.

Of course, what a guardian might consider antique was likely vastly different from what was considered antique by me.

Jiaotu untied the roll, flicking it open. It unfurled across the table, revealing a series of pockets. The largest held a stack of papers. Sticking out of two smaller pockets were the ornate hilt of a dagger, carved of white bone, and a large old-fashioned key.

Well, old-fashioned for the modern world. But again, pretty on par for a guardian.

"The deed," Jiaotu said, pressing his fingers to and rotating the leather portfolio toward me.

An inkwell and a handblown glass pen appeared next to my right hand. Black ink. The tip of the pen was gold.

I closed the memoir I was reading, shifting it to the side. Then I closed Infinity and set it on my lap, needing both hands free but still not quite trusting the library to not make a grab for the personal archive.

I pulled the stack of papers from the soft leather portfolio. It was thicker than I'd thought a transfer of ownership would be. My name...

My new name, Dusk Zhi Godfrey, was paired with Jiaotu's in the opening paragraph.

I read the deed. I didn't completely understand all the legal jargon—some of it, I had to translate from Latin—but I recognized enough to get the gist. Once I signed, I would legally own a piece of property and everything on or attached to that land. The previous and current street addresses were used to identify the property—as well as what I thought might have been ley line coordinates. It was in Dublin, as previously established.

I glanced at Jiaotu.

He raised an eyebrow at me.

I picked up the pen and initialed where prompted to do so at the bottom of each page. Then I signed and dated where my name was printed at the very end.

Magic laced into the ink seeped into the thick paper as it dried on each page.

Jiaotu turned the deed toward himself to go through the same process. When he scrawled his unreadable signature on the line next to mine, it was in a far messier hand than I expected.

The guardian then set his fingertips on the stack of papers, and a second stack appeared next to it, filled out in identical fashion. With another brush of his fingers, the duplicated set disappeared. Then he tucked the original contract back into the leather portfolio.

That hadn't been the illusion magic that only Jiaotu could wield like the demigod he was. Either that function had been built into the contract itself, or the guardian could make pristine duplicates that could pass for originals—legally and magically, no doubt. And which would presumably last a lifetime.

According to the papers I had just signed, the property would revert to the ownership of Jiaotu upon my death. Which, barring getting lost in the stacks and being declared dead at a young age, meant the duplication magic the guardian wielded would need to last centuries.

And would it last even beyond the guardian's lifespan? Because the mantle and name of Jiaotu were everlasting, no matter who accepted the responsibility of wearing them.

Observing that level of power being used so casually was staggering.

Sisu had forgotten he was pretending to be made out of stone, following the movement of our hands with an enraptured gaze. Though it was more likely the magic that stirred the air, echoing those movements, that enthralled the five-year-old.

Jiaotu removed the dagger from the leather roll. The entire weapon was carved out of the same white bone, not just the hilt. The guardian laid it before me, then stepped back and resumed sitting. Elbows set on the arms of the chair, fingers steepled. Watching me.

The exquisite dagger was inlaid with intricate swirls of gold that shifted under my gaze, tapering down to a deadly point. I waited for the golden swirls to settle into a discernible pattern. They didn't.

Aching to touch the weapon, to read it, I glanced over at Jiaotu.

I wasn't certain if I should thank him for the property. The contract we'd just signed made it clear it was a business transaction, part of the role I was taking on for the guardians.

"The key will unlock the main gate," Jiaotu finally said. "Make certain you have the deed on you, in hand or otherwise, when you step onto the property for the first time."

"Of course." I wasn't an idiot.

He smirked as if he could read my insolence in my tone. And maybe he could. Maybe I was only deluding myself when I thought I was hiding it.

"The transfer of ownership through the human world might take a couple of weeks, but the funds should be in your new ... bank accounts sooner than that." He waved his hand offishly. "Though according to Haoxin, you'll need to set that all up with your new name. I'll send some cash and other items to the house as well."

"Thank you."

He leveled a piercing gaze on me, eyes slightly narrowed.

I held that gaze steadily.

Sisu climbed into my lap. I tucked Infinity against my left thigh, and my brother curled up with his knees to his chest, head on my right arm. Slightly disconcertingly, my chair expanded to give him more legroom while also providing a built-in cushion for his head.

Jiaotu's gaze fell to his son.

I was dying to ask the guardian about the bone dagger.

I didn't.

"You are very young," he murmured, shifting back in his chair and crossing his legs.

I didn't answer. I was very young. Compared to a guardian dragon at least—even the third-youngest among the nine.

Silence stretched. Sisu's breathing deepened. He was falling asleep again. I had no idea how many hours we'd been in the library. Added to that, I had no idea how many hours we'd been in the nexus. When we left the dimensional pocket, it was possible that we would step directly back into the alley in Oslo only minutes after we'd exited it. Or ...

Or we might return home to find my mother waiting for us. Frantic because Sisu and I were now the ones who had disappeared for weeks. Though I had no doubt that the brownies of the nexus had already informed the brownies who ran our family estate of our whereabouts. We were their responsibility, after all.

I laid one hand on Sisu's hip, brushing my other fingertips against the symbols that edged Infinity's spine. Sleepy, peaceful energy hummed under my touch from both my brother and my personal archive.

Jiaotu blinked, then frowned, as if he'd been lost in thought. "The witches will likely send an emissary. The property and your ... sudden appearance as a Godfrey witch will be explained by an inheritance triggered on your twenty-fifth birthday. That was last week, wasn't it?"

I stared at the guardian, surprised that he knew my exact age or my date of birth.

"Am I wrong?" he said.

"No, guardian." I had received a few cards from relatives this year, and a book about Egyptian artifacts from Zeke. Mistress Brightshire had baked me a three-layer chocolate mousse cake. But it hadn't remotely been the same without my mother. No retelling of the events of the day of my birth while dusk settled over the day. No fireworks or games or dancing ... or laughter.

He nodded curtly. "What do you know of the Jiaotu bloodline?"

I glanced at him, then at Sisu, even more confused. "Just ... just what all dragons know. The guardians sectioned their core power into nine specific, complementary attributes when they divided the world into nine territories. To ... protect the world from magical incursions. Mostly. Jiaotu, the silver tongued, holds what is now loosely known as Northern Europe."

"The mantle of power is passed between guardian and apprentice," Jiaotu said. "Not necessarily along familial lines."

I nodded. "Right. There aren't enough dragons for only a child of Jiaotu to assume the mantle of Jiaotu when the time comes."

"Or the timing might be wrong. Another son of Jiaotu currently walks the earth, but he was lost at the time his mother passed her mantle to me."

"Another son..." I'd had no idea. I pressed my luck by asking a personal question I had no right to ask. "Older than you?"

"Warner was born to the present timeline before I was, yes."

I nodded, understanding that this earlier son of Jiaotu, Warner, was actually younger than the guardian. In the same way I was twenty-five, not sixty-nine.

"Jiaotu isn't known only for his silver tongue," the guardian said, waving one hand as if prompting me. "His ability to resolve most situations with ... words."

"Beguilement, you mean? Enchantment?"

He frowned. "No. Simple words." He nodded toward the books on the table. "Storytelling. Recollecting. I can access everything I've ever seen or read or heard."

Huh. So could I. To a certain extent, at least. And that wasn't a typical archivist trait.

"I can also recall the memories of she-before-me, and he-before-her. And so on."

I blinked. That was ... utterly overwhelming. How was that even possible to navigate? And ... and ... he knew so much! He ... he knew everything!

Wow.

No wonder my mother thought the guardian was worth—

Jiaotu leveled a piercing gaze on me, raising one eyebrow expectantly.

Right. I'd forgotten he was quizzing me for some unknown reason. "Jiaotu can also turn invisible," I said. "Like actual, impossible, no-footprints-in-the-snow invisibility."

He snorted. "That's a magical glamour. Same with walking in the rain and whatnot."

Well, that was disappointing.

Jiaotu shook his head at me. "I still exist."

"Matter cannot be destroyed."

"Exactly."

"And?"

"And…you are a master of illusion. An expert hunter, tracker."

"Finally we get to the point." He smiled through the otherwise harsh words, dropping his gaze to the blade. "Almost a millennia ago, Jiaotu-who-was hunted a deadly predator through her territory. An entity that could take on any form it wished, animal as well as human. And in doing so, it could also cloak itself from all her senses."

Being able to shape change so thoroughly that a creature disguised not only its physical appearance but its scent was rare, though not unheard of. Altering the scent or glow of its magic—to those sensitive enough to see the tiniest iota of magic, as all guardians could—was highly unusual. And cloaking the very essence of life that flowed through us all? I never would have believed it possible.

Of course, guardians were only summoned when all else failed. Or when all else was going to fail, according to Chi Wen the far seer.

"It was as perfect a hunter as she was," Jiaotu continued, his gaze remote.

Was he recalling the memory as if it were his own? Or could he somehow access just a summary of the events rather than reliving them in his mind's eye?

I fought off a wave of intense curiosity, another desperate rush to pepper him with questions. My right palm was itching madly. And I was utterly aware of both Infinity close at hand, and that the pen I'd used to sign the contract was still primed in the inkwell.

"Except the entity stole the energy it harnessed, instead of feeding it back into the universe as we dragons continually do." Jiaotu grimaced. "It decimated the villages it passed through, leaving nothing alive in its wake. I didn't know it until I absorbed her essence, but it became personal for Jiaotu. She even refused the help of Suanmi-who-was, who'd chased it north from her own territory."

My heart was beating rapidly. Not in fear but in pleased anticipation. Silver-tongued Jiaotu was sharing a story with me, a story of his guardian, his mentor. I gave in and set Infinity on the table, leaning over Sisu in my lap to grab the pen.

Jiaotu smirked at me, but didn't break the flow of his tale as he recounted the weeks that passed, and the unbearable cold and lack of food as Jiaotu-who-was herded her prey into the icy plains of the north. I placed the inked tip of the pen to the first page of Infinity, scrawling *Personal Notes: Jiaotu-who-was* across the top edge. My hand continued to move, ink flowing across the page, translating Jiaotu's words even before I absorbed them myself.

I flipped pages as needed, though the inked words would eventually absorb into the archive, forever stored in my personal notes section where I could recall and rewrite them as I willed.

Jiaotu continued his tale, recounting the story as if it was he who had crossed frozen rivers and swum through oceans, freezing and starving until the great prey was finally cornered on a small island far in the north. A wake of utter devastation marked its path for centuries after, the land deadened wherever it had stepped.

Sisu murmured in his sleep.

I realized that I'd been beguiled by Jiaotu, swept up into his tale. And that I didn't want it to end.

The guardian's piercing gaze fell to the dagger, and the spell broke. "They fought for days in their weakened state, until Jiaotu-who-was stabbed the creature through the heart."

"With this dagger?" I asked, hushed.

He smirked. "No. With a broken shard of its own leg. A femur, as she recounted it."

"Because claiming the entity's magic was the only way to truly vanquish it," I whispered. "And it had to be vanquished. Killed. Not collected or imprisoned, because of the threat it posed to the world."

Jiaotu smiled at me. A wide, pleased expression I'd never seen from him. A pride I'd never seen directed my way by anyone, except for the day my mother had presented me with Infinity. And, even then, her eyes had been filled with tears and her words backed by something I hadn't quite been able to figure out. Trepidation, maybe.

"The dagger?" I asked, already knowing the answer.

"The femur reformed."

I stared at the priceless, one-of-a-kind magical artifact sitting on the table before me. It was carved out of the femur of a long-dead entity who had taken on a guardian dragon and almost won.

"It goes with the estate," Jiaotu said, his tone suddenly flippant. Even a touch harsh.

I had no idea what he was talking about.

He huffed. "It is part of your inheritance. I'm descended from Jiaotu-who-was on my father's side. He was her grandchild. So I am of her bloodline as well as her chosen apprentice. At the time of my ascension, as far as we knew, my father and I were Jiaotu's sole blood relatives." He paused, as if wanting to give me time to absorb the new influx of information.

Sisu's section of the family tree, previously left blank above Jiaotu's entry as his father, had suddenly grown another branch. Not only was Jiaotu his father, she had also been his great-great-grandmother.

No wonder he was almost stronger and faster than me at age five.

Of course, he ran everywhere and climbed anything climbable, while I preferred to walk. So it was possible that simply honing those abilities had something to do with it. Magic was like that. It both hated being ignored and abhorred a vacuum.

"Among other things, the dagger and the estate in Dublin passed to me when I took up the mantle of Jiaotu. And now I deed them both to you for life. It is not within my power to gift them beyond that."

The property in Dublin had been owned by Jiaotu-who-was?

"My father lived out his last years in Dublin..." A wry smile flitted over the guardian's face. "He and Suanmi were...close. She's been trying to purchase the estate from me for years. The stasis spells that now protect it will hold only until you use the key."

Unable to hold his gaze with my mind whirling, I stared down at Infinity. At some point, I'd stopped taking notes, though I was still holding the pen resting on the now-blank page, ink pooling from its tip. Since Infinity absorbed magic along with words, the archive wouldn't mind the ink blots.

A few months after he'd recovered enough to work as my mother's apprentice in Giza, Zeke had whispered a rumor to me that Jiaotu and Suanmi were lovers, or had been at one point. I had assumed the relationship predated Jiaotu meeting my mother, and Sisu's birth. Not that I expected dragons to be faithful without a formalized bond—which, as far as I knew, my mother and Jiaotu didn't have. But it seemed doubtful that a guardian dragon would share her lover, whether or not he was also a guardian.

"It is a powerful weapon," Jiaotu murmured into the magic-filled hush surrounding us. His gaze had fallen to the dagger. "But meant to be wielded by a smaller hand. By a woman."

"I don't understand," I mumbled, overwhelmed by the gift. Signing the contract might have felt like a business transaction—professional recompense for the new life the guardians wanted me to undertake. But the dagger was…something else. Something intimate, something with huge expectations tied to it.

The expectation that I was worthy of wielding it.

Worthy of being tasked by the guardian dragons in the first place. Of sitting across from Jiaotu and gaining even just a glimpse into his mind, his memories.

The guardian of Northern Europe stood up, set his hands on the table to either side of the bone dagger, and leaned over to press a kiss to my forehead. "For you, Dusk. To guard you, as needed."

Magic shifted between us. I stilled under its touch, accepting it, absorbing it.

"You will need to claim the dagger. It shifts shape according to its wielder's needs."

"Really?" I was aware that I sounded breathless, and a little idiotic. Also, a little confused. Jiaotu had already said the weapon was meant for a smaller hand, and shifting shape seemed to contradict that idea. "That's … that's …" I'd run out of words. For the first time in my life, my mind was just blank.

"Keep it with you, Dusk," Jiaotu said, his tone deadly serious. Words laced with magic. "At all times. Eventually, you will be able to recall it to you with a mere thought. But for now, heed me."

I gazed up at him. His expression was almost pained. Harsh, frowning. As if he wanted to say more.

"Yes, guardian."

Flicking his gaze over me, he said quietly, "That's your mother's sweater."

I touched the colorful yoke. "Yes."

Then Jiaotu reached across the wide table, scooped the sleeping Sisu out of my lap, and turned away. "I will lead you back home."

Numbed by the immensity of the guardian's gift, I ran my fingers along the hilt of the dagger. It thrummed with power. I stopped short of reading its history, though. I was already too overwhelmed. The dagger would be best digested in tiny sips and glimpses.

My heart was hammering for an entirely different reason now, smothered by a crushing fear of not being ready for the responsibility of owning such an artifact. Of not being powerful enough to protect it. To even envision myself using it.

Of wielding what a guardian herself had once wielded, had once created.

Sisu woke up as Jiaotu disappeared between the towering bookshelves. The books that had been piled on the table rose into the air and were whisked away.

I grabbed the dagger, sliding it back into the soft leather portfolio, along with the key and the deed. Then I rolled it all up and tucked it into my backpack. I grabbed Sisu's backpack and ran after the guardian.

It would take me days to process the story of the bone dagger, to even begin to understand the nuances of the entire interaction from the meeting with the guardians to tea with Jiaotu. But as I caught up with the white-blond guardian now carrying my brother on his shoulders—and deftly sidestepping every attempt Sisu made to swipe random books and objects from the shelves—I was finally able to slow my pace and my mind.

I realized that one of the nine most powerful beings in the world believed I needed a magical artifact of epic power to face the future I had just accepted.

And even as trepidation soured my stomach, that was utterly thrilling.

CHAPTER FOUR

SOMEHOW WE STEPPED DIRECTLY FROM THE LIBRARY into the heart of the nexus, ending up facing the white-and-gray door that I was fairly certain led to Jiaotu's territory. And, when focused on a specific point, our family estate.

Sisu, still atop his father's shoulders, leaned deeply to the side to brush his fingers against the relief carved into the door, tracing the lines of a long tooth. Up close, I could see other animals tucked around the main pairing of the snarling wolf and the striking raptor.

"You don't shape change," I blurted before I'd thought the question through. "I mean … Jiaotu doesn't take the form of an animal … a wolf … or eagle …" I trailed off into the silence, dropping my gaze from Jiaotu's piercing blue eyes.

"No," he said, lifting Sisu from his shoulders and setting him on the marble floor. "That talent lies with Bixi."

I tried to help Sisu on with his backpack, but my brother wiggled away from me, slipping the pack on frontwards instead. Then he unzipped the outer pocket, peering into it and grinning. "Hello."

I'd let him keep the golden egg.

"You were wondering about the carvings," Jiaotu finally said. "The animal motif."

"Yes," I said, turning my attention back to the door. "I understand that the dominant Adept species in Northern Europe was once the shapeshifters, and werewolves specifically." Human industrialization had long ago devastated the wilds of Europe—the territories that had once been held by the shifters. Even among those who had started new packs in North America, werewolves heavily outnumbered the other animal forms.

"Along with the wily witches." Jiaotu's tone turned wry. "Though the vampire that Suanmi finds so amusing wiped entire generations of necromancers from Europe, the witches kept him at bay with a pact of fealty."

I blinked at him. "The witches would have had to offer a powerful vampire something very … valuable."

Jiaotu nodded, grimacing distastefully. Then his gaze settled back on the door. "They sacrificed their second-born children."

"Sacrificed? You mean they gave him, and the vampire shiver specifically, their children?"

"Once they reached a certain age. Jiaotu-who-was drove him from her territory, and Suanmi keeps him in check now. Though I have no idea why she doesn't just destroy him. Balance, perhaps. But more likely boredom …" He touched the door, stroking the line of the raptor's wing before allowing his arm to fall at his side. "The design has changed since I became Jiaotu. All the doors do."

"The European shifters are … rebuilding?"

"Perhaps." Apparently done with the conversation, Jiaotu laid his hand on Sisu's head. Power shifted under his palm.

Sisu raised his chin, giggling.

As far as I could sense, nothing happened to or around my brother. So most likely a glamour, then. Not to change Sisu's appearance, but to make his magic pass for witch power more easily. I'd almost forgotten that the guardian Haoxin had insisted on it, along with the deed to the property and the extra cash Jiaotu was sending.

The guardian lifted his hand from Sisu's head. My brother looked down at his hands, then up at me. "Am I still me? Me Sisu? Or ..." His face practically exploded with joy. "Someone else? Oh! Oh! I have a great name picked out!"

"It's to make your magic read as a witch," I said. "Remember?"

Sisu's eyes widened. "Right." He looked at his father, then down at his feet. "A witch. We're going to move to Dublin. Without Mom. And I have a new name already."

I opened my mouth to address the Mom comment.

Jiaotu cut me off. "No," he said, looming over my little brother. "Your real name will always be Sisu Jiaotuson. Unless you elect to one day wear a guardian mantle, you will never be anyone else. My son." A slow grin transformed Jiaotu's face. A teasing, playful smile.

Until this day—first in the council chamber, then the library, then now—I'd never seen the guardian of Northern Europe smile. Smirk, yes. Smile, no.

"But," Jiaotu continued, "while you are helping your sister with her new position, it will be a little like changing your face, except the glamour is invisible."

"Pretend," Sisu whispered reverently.

Jiaotu touched him lightly on the head. "Exactly." The guardian then turned to me, his expression cooling as he did.

Not necessarily angry at me. More as if he was angry at the situation? At being...manipulated?

I remembered the guardian of Western Europe looking pleased numerous times during the final deliberations with the other guardians, as if she'd gotten her way. But with what?

Wait.

Haoxin had suggested that having an archivist live among the Adept was Suanmi's idea, her so-called scheme. And Jiaotu had been the one to request the guardian quorum. But for what? To stop Suanmi from appointing me specifically? Or appointing just any archivist? To protect me? From what? From...the guardian of Western Europe herself? That didn't make any sense.

Maybe it was simply that Jiaotu hadn't wanted me to be solely under Suanmi's control. If she'd assigned me to London or Berlin, would an estate have come with the offer? Or would I have been left to figure that all out on my own? And what would that have meant for Sisu? Would I have been forced to give him up?

"Guardian?" I murmured, my mind once again reeling. "Is there anything else I need to know...about being your vassal?"

He smirked. "You're worried about the conditions of your homage and allegiance?"

I flushed, but that was the actual definition of being a vassal.

"You are Sisu's sister," he said. "That is all I...want you to be. For the near future."

The near future? On a scale from one to a hundred, how many years did the guardian count as near?

Jiaotu smirked at me, as if he could tell what I was thinking.

And again, maybe I didn't hide my snark as well as I thought I did. "I only ask because the guardian of Western Europe—"

Jiaotu shook his head to stop me, then looked down at Sisu. "What did I tell you about the doors?"

Sisu looked utterly panicked for a moment, then he grinned. "That they have ears!"

Ah, okay. Message received. Don't mention Suanmi, or anything else I didn't want overheard, when in the heart of the nexus.

"And why did I tell you this?" Jiaotu prompted.

"Because I can call you from here," Sisu said obligingly. "If I'm in the nexus and can't find you."

Jiaotu flicked his gaze to me, raising one eyebrow.

Instead of huffing indignantly at the suggestion that I needed prompting to absorb his none-too-subtle teaching moment, I nodded. Though under other circumstances, I might have questioned how Sisu or I were meant to gain access to the nexus in the first place, let alone use the door to summon him.

I'd really been mouthy enough already.

Plus I really, really liked the bone dagger, and really, really didn't want to do anything to anger the guardian who'd given it to me.

Jiaotu snorted. "The glamour won't hold on you, Dusk," he said coolly. "It will take to Sisu slightly more strongly, as his magic is less formed. But your personal magic will wear against it. I can try to smooth the cracks as they appear, of course..." He trailed off, flicking his gaze over my face as if assessing me. Or perhaps assessing my so-called cracks ahead of time.

"Your guidance is much appreciated, guardian," I said, falling back on my best behavior. I was suddenly weary. That was why I was being snarky, even if just in my own head.

Yes, I was bone-weary, as if I'd been up for days.

And maybe I had.

Sisu curled his hand into mine.

I wanted to look down at him, to reassure him, but I also didn't want to break the guardian's remote gaze. So I squeezed my brother's fingers instead, smiling when he bumped his shoulder into my leg gently.

Jiaotu blinked, as if the slight movement had woken him. He nodded once, then pressed his forefinger and middle finger to the center of my forehead.

Energy shifted between us, though it didn't spread over me as I'd expected.

"A dragon passing for a witch," Jiaotu sneered, dropping his hand.

"I'll do my best," I said seriously.

"As will I!" Sisu exclaimed exuberantly.

Jiaotu laughed quietly. "You are your mother's children." Then his expression stiffened, as if he'd upset himself by his own mention of my mother. "I'll send what I've promised when you've claimed the estate."

"Thank you, guardian. Should I...I will...send you a copy of my personal journal? Monthly? Or perhaps twice yearly?" A heavily edited copy, maybe.

Reporting directly to the guardians wasn't something that had been covered in my training so far. I'd never even heard of an archivist being tasked directly to one guardian before, let alone the four who had pretty much just claimed me. Jiaotu, Suanmi, Bixi, and Pulou. And maybe even with Haoxin possibly in the mix. Not that the preservation of knowledge wasn't important, but the guardians were pretty busy saving the world and worrying about the future. The archivists preserved the past.

Except for me.

Okay, I had just snapped those pieces of the evolving puzzle together. Honestly, I was such an idiot sometimes. This was why I really, really preferred books more than people, more than conversation. In a book, the plot was usually laid out concisely, and...

Jiaotu was staring at me, one eyebrow raised belligerently. No. Guardian dragons weren't belligerent. Well, maybe they were, but that wasn't for me to say.

"I'm sorry, guardian," I blurted. "I'm quite tired, and —"

He waved me off. "I'll accept reports, if they are even needed, in person. When I visit Sisu."

Well, that made more sense. I actually wasn't even certain how I'd send him a written report in the first place.

"I will also contact you if I hear of or from your mother," Jiaotu continued. "Unfortunately, if she is walking through time, I cannot seek her myself. That path is closed to guardians."

That was definitely news to me. Though it made sense. Guardians held a lot of magic, so one misstep in the past and...

Jiaotu was smirking at me.

Again.

I snapped my mouth shut. Yes, it had been hanging open. "Thank you, guardian."

He nodded. "Go, Dusk. You've drained and replenished more magic than you usually would when filling your archive. The nexus is generous with its energy, but it is demanding as well."

A golden light edged the door before me. Then the door itself seemed to dissolve, opening into a whirling vortex of power.

I took Sisu's hand.

Jiaotu touched his son's head once, gently. "Be good for your sister." Then the guardian turned to me. "Think of your front door, Dusk. Of the feel of the stone of the entranceway under your feet."

I nodded, stepping forward and into the tunnel of energy. For a brief moment, I swore I felt Jiaotu's fingers brush my shoulder, just as he'd touched Sisu to bid farewell. But then the portal had us in its grasp, and I focused on the image of the main house at the family estate, focused on stepping through onto—

White marble turned into light-gray granite under my feet. I blinked away the magic clouding my sight, finding myself staring at a sweeping staircase and eclectic artwork occupying every available vertical surface.

The house felt the same around me—a dense but benign energy anchored firmly into the earth. There was no hint of my mother in the front hall. Even her residual magic had faded. From my ability to sense it, at least. It had gone months ago. Except for in her rooms.

Home.

For a little while, at least.

"Finally," a gravelly voice muttered. "I thought I was going to have to hold dinner. Again."

A stout woman, standing about a meter high, stood with her hands on her hips in the doorway to the dining room, glaring at us.

Mistress Brightshire.

The head brownie of our family estate gazed at us with narrowed eyes, then sniffed dismissively. Her exceedingly curly light-brown hair was braided, falling all the way to her lower back. Her apron was bright-blue linen and ruffled at the edges. "Playing with the guardians will only bring trouble down around your heads, you know."

"I know."

She sighed heavily, then brushed her hands together. "Fine, fine. You never did listen." Then she disappeared.

I listened!

I was a good—

"Wait," Sisu howled. "I'm starving!" He dumped his backpack on the floor, taking off toward the kitchen.

Sighing internally, I scooped up Sisu's pack and started for the stairs. Food was a good idea, no matter how tired I was. Then a hot shower. Then bed.

Some part of me had hoped Mom would be home on our return. Really, really hoped.

Ignoring a sudden aching need to talk to someone, specifically Mom, I realized that I had no idea how many days we'd lost to the nexus. What felt like a few hours might have been a week, or even weeks. The calendar in the library would let me know for certain. But Mistress Brightshire choosing to appear anywhere but in the kitchen told me that even though she'd been notified of our presence in the nexus, we'd been gone for longer than she liked.

I climbed the stairs, dropping Sisu's backpack in his room, then heading for my own room. I might not have needed a bathroom while hanging out with guardian dragons, but I really needed one now.

And even I had to admit that it was seriously creepy how all that magic—the nexus and its so-called generosity—somehow also kept bodily functions in check.

After getting Sisu into bed—he'd insisted on sleeping with the new sword and the golden egg, though I managed to negotiate the weapon onto the side table with the promise that I'd spar with him in the morning—I carefully folded my mother's sweater and tucked it onto a shelf in my closet. I was hoping the brownies would let me keep it now that I'd excavated it from Mom's substantial clothing collection.

Smoothing my fingers over the colorful yoke, I recalled Jiaotu recognizing the sweater.

A sweater that I could have sworn my mother hadn't pulled out of storage since she'd crossed back into the present day twenty-three years ago. With a two-year-old in tow. Me.

Mom had been wearing the sweater the day I was born. I knew because when she recounted the tale of my birth—as she had every single birthday, excepting the one she'd now missed—she focused on that sweater as the reason she'd been pulled through the stacks in London. Specifically, into 1952. A magical surge, triggering early labor, had enveloped her while she'd been authenticating an artifact in the stacks of the British Museum, the Dunkirk coven's seat of power.

Because the sweater had been knitted by a Dunkirk witch in 1952, that was the year Mom had stumbled into, then given birth to me. That witch was a friend my mother made when she'd apprenticed at the London archive—when she'd lived through the year 1952 for the first time, in her original personal timeline. Mom had—repeatedly—mentioned how much trouble the witches had to go through to keep us hidden from her past self while she'd tried to figure out how to get us back to the present time.

Though the ability was rare even among archivists, shifting through time created havoc with more than just family trees. And the archivists who held the talent to slip through time often developed strategies to avoid causing too much damage to the timeline. My birth was the first time my mother had time slipped on her own, but she'd previously done so with her mother, Ruth, and her Uncle

Beckett. When Ruth slipped through time, she never left the confines of the archive she would travel within, not if she could help it. And Beckett had developed a unique timepiece to help navigate the dangers of moving back through history.

So when had Jiaotu seen Mom wearing the sweater? I frowned, then shook off the odd thought. Who knew anything for certain with a guardian? Jiaotu might have seen a picture, or maybe my mother had simply told him the tale in vivid detail, as she was prone to doing.

I sighed, crossing into the bedroom and tugging the curtains closed. It was full dark. The moon hadn't made an appearance. The rolling acres of our family estate were always pristinely groomed, including the vegetable gardens and orchard. But the wilds of the mountains of Norway were only a step beyond the back property boundary. Tomorrow, I would take Sisu for a hike to burn some energy—enough energy that I could then get him focused on packing for Dublin. Hopefully.

The calendar in the library informed me that we'd lost two weeks to the nexus. It would be late October before I managed to start my new job. But instead of standing frozen in place by the weight of my ever-expanding to-do list, I turned off the side table light and climbed into bed.

I had left the bone dagger on my writing desk.

I felt the magical artifact the moment I turned my back on it, radiating warmth and encouragement. And since rationally, I knew that daggers couldn't emanate emotions, I took that feeling as a sign of how my mind—my actual brain—was interpreting Jiaotu's instructions and the magical binding that had come with the gift.

I climbed out of bed, grabbing the entire worn leather portfolio and tucking it under my pillow. I would deal with claiming the weapon—whatever that actually meant—and feeding the deed for the property into Infinity for safekeeping in the morning.

And apparently, I was going to need to contact an Adept lawyer—I had a life to relocate.

A week later, I was halfway to the library with the last two letters I'd been hesitating to send tucked into Infinity, when I felt a presence deeper within the house. Turning on my heel, I crossed the hall to greet our newly arrived guest.

When it was only Sisu and me at home, we ate in the kitchen nook. But I spotted a small buffet set up on the sideboard through the archway to the more formal dining room. Mistress Brightshire had—no doubt eagerly—pulled out the silver chafing dishes, the coffee urn and teapot, plus china plates and teacups for our guest.

I stepped within the dining room.

A dark-blond, golden-skinned dragon was seated near the center of the long, dark-wood antique dining table. An empty bowl, likely having previously contained fruit salad, sat next to his left elbow. His head was bowed over a dark-blue leather-bound book with gilded pages—his deceptively sleek and unadorned magical archive. He was dressed in a black sweater, sleeves shoved up to expose his forearms, and old blue jeans.

Zeke.

My great-great-uncle, though technically he was adopted and appeared to be in his mid to late twenties. And that technicality, plus the distance between us on the family tree, meant there was nothing to prevent me from inviting him to my bed. Which I had. On numerous occasions, since the time he'd been rescued and rehabilitated at the estate under Mom's care.

My stomach flipped. Unfortunately, it then soured rather than warming with desire.

One of the unsent notes currently tucked into Infinity was meant for Zeke. I had hesitated to contact him sooner, because I knew he was going to be pissy about the guardians' offer and my acceptance. Though he was generally averse to any abrupt change, Zeke specifically had other plans for me. Or, more accurately, for my body.

Unfortunately, my interest in Zeke was much more...loosely defined. Playful. Even sexy at times. It was fun to sneak around at the estate or for a weekend in London, but...well, honestly, if I stayed with him any longer, his need to control every minute and moment started to drive me a little crazy.

That was completely and utterly shallow of me, given everything he'd been through. But it was just the way it was. For now at least.

I had turned down Zeke's so-called plan as definitively as I knew how to when dealing with a family member I couldn't actually break up with—by kicking him out of my bed and only replying to his letters with polite but minimal details.

Moving to Dublin might have been coming at the best possible time, actually. I couldn't be accused of running away like some coward, but Zeke also couldn't just cross through the stacks of the Giza archives and show up for breakfast either. It was the power of the family estate library that opened that doorway for him. And only because Mom had shown him the way.

"Why is there a pile of trunks and boxes in the foyer?" Zeke asked without looking up from his book.

I crossed to the sideboard, finding spinach egg benedict, crispy hash browns, and buttered toast under the domed lids of the silver chafing dishes. Zeke's favorites. Mistress Brightshire adored having multiple people to cook for.

I was pleased to find my favorite grilled chicken sausages under the final lid. "I've been reassigned."

Zeke glanced at me questioningly. I could suddenly feel the weight of the letters tucked into Infinity in my left hand—and that weight felt a lot like guilt about not having written him sooner. I set Infinity to the side, quickly serving myself, including a small bowl of the fruit salad.

"Where?"

"The National Museum of Ireland in Dublin. Head curator of the magical archive."

He frowned. "There wasn't someone more qualified?"

"Apparently not," I snapped.

Zeke huffed, closing his own archive to stand and cross to the sideboard. He cupped his hand under my elbow, leaning into me.

I didn't turn my head, so his kiss brushed my cheek rather than my lips. The contact—on my elbow and my face—left a touch of magic in its wake. And, for the first time, I understood why so many Adepts were reluctant to touch each other. The residual magic wasn't malicious, but it was oddly intrusive.

Zeke frowned slightly, but he dropped his hand and served himself a plate.

I retrieved Infinity, sitting across from him at the middle of the table. Even without our elders present, we deferred to our natural positions. Mom would have sat at the head of the table had she been home.

Grandparents or Aunt Josephine or Great-Uncle Jamal would have been flanking her if any of them were in residence.

Though Zeke outwardly accepted his junior role in the family, he inwardly chafed at it. A fact I'd been unaware of until he laid out what the next twenty-five years of my life was going to look like, from his perspective.

And it wasn't as if I didn't understand. Zeke, aka Ezekiel, had been born in 1632. He'd been lost in 1711. Found in 2016. Making him eighty-two years old by the accounting of how long he'd actually lived in the world. But he'd spent another three hundred and five years trapped in his sister's spelled copy of *The Iliad*, during which he fought for his life every day but hadn't aged a year. Now, though he hadn't been aware that quite so much time had passed, to his mind, he should have been a senior member of the family. Running an archive, or at least a renowned collector.

Instead, he was still years away from his majority and apprenticed to Mom.

Zeke returned to his seat, flicking his napkin and setting it over his knee.

We ate in silence until he asked, "Is the packing the reason Sisu is avoiding me?"

"How do you know he's avoiding you?"

"I came through the library just after dawn," Zeke said. "He was already up, but he took off when I greeted him."

"He's nervous about the move."

Zeke paused, a forkful of potatoes halfway to his mouth. "He's … you're taking him with you?"

"Why wouldn't I?" I asked testily. Apparently, I wasn't going to feel guilty for very long.

Sisu had been a large part of the conversation that Zeke had forced upon me the last time we'd been skin to skin. That was some sort of a betrayal, wasn't it? Having your immediate future rearranged in a moment of such intimacy?

Zeke looked at me for a long moment.

I just focused on my breakfast. I had no idea when I was going to eat my next home-cooked meal, unless I learned to make more than cinnamon buns and cold plates. A tiny fissure of shock ran through me as I realized I was going to have to shop, for groceries, for … household … supplies …

"He's not your responsibility," Zeke said quietly. "How will you take over an archive while taking care of your brother? He has a father. A father with a vast amount of resources—"

"Are you here with news of my mother?"

Zeke sighed. "No. I'm here to check up on you."

"A letter would have sufficed."

"I've written."

"I've answered."

"Not sufficiently."

Sisu went barreling past the open doorway. Possibly carrying a chair that belonged in his room over his head.

Zeke threw his napkin on the table, pushing his half-eaten food away. "Is this because I asked you about your plans? About the possibility of children?"

I didn't remember any actual questions being asked during our last face-to-face conversation. Just a lot of laying out of those so-called plans punctuated with meticulous timelines.

"Yes, Zeke," I said, heavy on the sarcasm. "I begged the guardian dragons to appoint me to the head curator position in Dublin because you'd outlined a detailed breeding program. For me."

He flushed. Then like any good archivist, he latched onto the most important detail. "Guardian dragons? Plural?"

Still trying to savor what was starting to feel like my last meal, I tugged the letters I'd written the previous night out of Infinity, flicking the thinner envelope across the table. I had taken the time to write, then rewrite, a concise accounting of the offer and what it entailed. Including the facts that I'd be living in Dublin, rather than commuting, and that I'd have no library for Zeke or any of my other relatives to use to cross through and visit me.

A tiny pit of despair opened in my stomach at that thought. Sisu and I might have spent the last eleven months mostly on our own, with only training sessions and visits with Zeke for outside company, but I wasn't actually well versed in being alone, or lonely. The family estate was filled with magical creatures, and gardens, and a massive library of books and artifacts to explore and experience.

Except for Sisu, I was going to be alone—really alone—in Dublin.

I had no idea how to deliberately make friends, or to work with someone I wasn't related to. My previous friendships outside of family members—or acquaint-anceships at least—had just occurred … well, naturally. We would meet during a training session or a grand-scale celebration, such as the Chinese New Year the family had spent in Shanghai two years ago. And we would enjoy each other's company for as long as that lasted.

But how was I going to make friends while pretending to be a witch? Wasn't honesty supposed to be a fundamental aspect of solid relationships?

I was thinking about it too much.

Magic had already told me—by delivering the branch of cherry blossoms—that I was on the correct path. I just had to walk it now.

Zeke slowly reached for the letter, smoothing his fingers across his name where I'd inked it in my favorite brown-and-speckled-gold ink. The gesture was somehow filled with reverence.

And my stomach curdled. Again.

"It wasn't a...breeding program," he murmured, tucking the unread letter into his personal archive. "It was a logical offer, taking into account your level of training and position, factoring in how long it would take for your career to advance. Apparently, I didn't have all the information. I'm simply...terrible at expressing myself."

I sighed heavily. "You're an arrogant asshole who thinks he's better educated and more worldly than me. Even now, you're sitting across from me telling me what to do with my own brother."

He blinked, anger flickering over his face. "Why sleep with me, then?"

I threw my hands up. "Which time? When you were healing? When you were playful and it was fun? Why not?"

He flushed. "We have responsibilities. At least I have."

I stood, scooping up Infinity and the second letter, and abandoning my last chicken sausage.

Zeke grumbled something in Ancient Greek that I didn't bother to translate. He lapsed into the language he'd spent three hundred years trapped within when he was angry or overwhelmed. When Mom had first brought him home, he couldn't speak English at all. I hadn't had Infinity to translate then, so I'd slowly learned the language just to help Zeke communicate.

I would read to him from his mother's journals, painstakingly translating each word from English while he'd clenched a sword or a staff and stood at the windows of whatever room we were within. Staring out at the estate, expecting to be attacked at any moment.

Feeling like an asshole myself, I paused in the doorway. Then I stepped back around the table to retrieve my last sausage. I took a bite, crossing around to gaze down at Zeke.

He laid his hand on his archive, sighing. "This changes things."

I snorted. "Who else am I going to breed with, Zeke?"

He looked up at me, frowning slightly. "You'll have options. Lots of options. You are beautiful and strong, powerful even if untrained."

He had to add that last bit. Sighing, I shook my head. "So will you."

He opened his mouth to argue.

I took another bite of the sausage and left the dining room. We'd had all the parts of that conversation that I wanted to have already, and I hated repeating myself.

Zeke and I were a technically perfect match. Genetically distant, but somewhat close in age. Lived age, at any rate. Both of us archivists, though I understood that Zeke's birth parents had been warriors. Our coupling, with the hopes of actually breeding, would have been encouraged by our elders—sometime in the next hundred years or so.

But Zeke wasn't interested in waiting that long to 'move on with his life,' as he'd phrased it.

And I wasn't interested in formalizing our relationship. Yet.

Even acknowledging it to my mother—had she been at home—would have taken all the fun out of it. Though I had no doubt that our more intimate interactions hadn't been as well hidden as we thought they were.

Zeke was intelligent and resourceful. And, after a little training, a considerate lover.

But overall, the relationship was a little boring. Predictable.

Expected.

So decades from now—assuming I wanted to breed—I could.

But I was a little busy at the moment.

I had wanted more, and it had just been handed to me. Literally. So now I was going to have to deal with it all. Zeke could wait. Or he wouldn't.

That didn't change what my next steps needed to be.

I ran my fingers along the spines of centuries' worth of books as I crossed through the library toward my mother's desk. Different tenors of energy tingled across my skin—witch, sorcerer, necromancer, and dragon magic bound in leather and paper. The heavy drapes were open, sunlight streaming in to highlight the golden shade of the oak flooring and furniture.

An ornate oak desk was centered directly across from the unlit stone fireplace. A smaller table sat on the right of the desk, currently piled high with books that needed to be shelved, personally archived by my mother.

That was how I knew for certain that she was still alive. More books kept appearing, one or two a month, meaning my mother was still actively feeding her personal archive—the black-leather tome that was her own version of my Infinity.

The new additions to the library were coated in enough magic that I couldn't touch them.

Well, I couldn't touch them … much.

When Mom died, all her boundary and containment wards would die with her. That energy wouldn't just disappear in an instant, of course, but it would fade. Unfortunately, no new books had appeared in the library in the time we'd been in Oslo and the nexus. And yes, I had memorized the piles.

A noticeboard lined with burgundy velvet hung on the wall behind the desk, tucked between the overly full bookshelves that ran the entire length of the wall. The narrow table set underneath the noticeboard's gilded frame and the three shelves whose contents I'd packed into my boxes were the only empty surfaces in the entire room.

Not quite ready to execute my final task before leaving the estate, I abandoned the desk to gaze out the far window. The day was bright, sunny. The maple and oak trees were starting to turn color, their leaves yellowing as they did before they turned vibrant shades of red, orange, and brown.

I would miss autumn on the estate. It was my favorite season.

I'd never lived anywhere else. Not that I distinctly remembered, anyway. My exceptional memory didn't date back to before I was two.

I cradled Infinity to my chest, thinking about the leaves now pressed between the archive's pages. Bright red from the Japanese maples … golden brown from the oak that shadowed the pond … all brought to me with a whisper of magic, and therefore dutifully collected and preserved by me. Though to what end, I still had no idea.

Just like I had no idea what the next few days, the next months, would bring. Or how well I would navigate my new position, my new life.

Archivists weren't big on the new. We preferred to dwell in the old. Traversing well-worn paths, upholding traditions, preserving the past.

Infinity stirred under my hand—a slight hum of energy that felt like a question, as if it were responding to my inner turmoil.

Apparently, I was being dramatic.

The magical archive settled, slipping back into its state of slumbering awareness. I still didn't know if it was the incident in Oslo, exposure to the magic of the nexus, or all the information I'd fed into it that had affected Infinity so profoundly. I just hoped that the archive would continue to recover.

The local newspapers I'd managed to get my hands on from Oslo had reported the power outage as large but contained. A few blown transformers. Cause still unknown.

Zeke stepped into the library, immediately crossing to the noticeboard. As any archivist tied to our household would do. But I knew the only letters attached to the burgundy velvet were addressed to my mother.

"I should shelve these," Zeke murmured.

I forced myself to turn away from the window and the melancholy I was stoking. Zeke was standing behind the side table piled high with my mother's new acquisitions. His hands were in his pockets, head bowed.

"Can you?" I asked. "I can't."

"Actually, you're right. Anything she's collecting for the main archive should appear there." He looked at me then. "Will you be able to write?"

"I'm always able to write."

He huffed, shaking his head. "I mean, do you know how to set up a noticeboard of your own?"

I didn't, but it was already on my list of things to figure out. I closed the space between us until we were standing on either side of the large oak desk. "Your thoughts are appreciated."

Zeke grimaced, crossing around the desk to pull a piece of blank paper from the top drawer. He retrieved a fountain pen from his back pocket that hadn't been there a moment before. That was another archivist talent I hadn't manifested yet—pulling a personalized pen from its last known location with a mere thought. Zeke could do the same with his archive as well.

He jotted down a series of runes. Two separate arcs. "I only know the anchor points for the Giza archives and the estate," he said, not looking up. The deep-black ink he used glittered with a silvery tone that I knew was platinum. It was receptive to Zeke's magic.

"So ... I ink those runes on the back of my noticeboard," I said. "And any note pinned here or in Giza, and addressed to me, will then transfer to my board. Once I set it up." Once I tied it to me. How? I had no idea.

"Yes." Zeke capped his pen, leaving the freshly inked paper on the desk.

"How ..." I faltered. I hated appearing ignorant in front of Zeke. But some things I had just taken for granted, like how the noticeboard worked. "How will the note addressed to me know where to arrive? Know that I'm in Dublin, not here?" I nodded toward the board behind Zeke, where four notes to my mother waited. "Mom's notes pile up here, not wherever she currently is."

He followed my gaze, touching the bottom corner of the noticeboard, then rubbed his forehead. "That's...that's just how the magic works. Your inherent magic."

"But there must be mail piling up in Giza for Mom as well," I whispered, a hollow point opening up in my chest.

"Addressed with her title, yes."

Ah, that was the difference. But... "You get mine in Giza...but when you're living here, your mail appears here, all addressed to Zeke. No title."

He smirked. "You intend the letter to be delivered to me. And so it is."

I frowned, not liking that explanation.

Zeke's smile widened. He shoved his hands in his front pockets again and wandered around the desk, leaning next to me. "Not everything can be known, little archivist. Some things you take on faith."

"I know," I said stiffly. And I did. I just preferred the proven, the verifiable. Even if just to see whether I could break the verifiable rules myself.

"Trissa is obviously traveling through time or in a pocket dimension, so her letters sit here, awaiting her return."

"And the books that she feeds into her archive?" I nodded toward the pile on the side table. "She can send those but not a note?" I sounded just a little bit angry, surprising myself.

Zeke smirked at me knowingly. "That's the power of her archive. Our archives. Noticeboards are minor bits of power. Tiny anchor points."

"Plus," I murmured, easing my own ire by acknowledging another truth, "she could have no idea how much time has passed. Sisu and I were in the nexus for what felt like a few hours, and it turned out to be two weeks."

"Yes. Exactly." Zeke cast his gaze to the floor, all traces of his playful smirk evaporated. "I had...no idea..."

He'd had no idea that three hundred years had passed while he'd been trapped in *The Iliad*. I brushed my fingers against his forearm, drawing his attention back to me.

He blinked, then nodded. "I won't be able to walk through the archives in Dublin."

"Jamal did, didn't he? When he was called in to help the witches?"

Zeke grimaced. "And that worked out so well for him."

"You mean it isn't a talent of yours, to forge new pathways." Zeke could walk anywhere he'd been previously taken. He could travel from the estate to Giza, but only because my mother had carved that path with him. Same with taking me to London six months ago. He'd gone there first with my mother.

I had no talent to open doorways myself, not even after I'd been shown the way.

He nodded, slowly reaching up to cup my face, turning it more fully toward him. He barely touched me, as if concerned that I would pull away, but I relented.

His deep-brown eyes flicked to my mouth, then back up to meet my own, offering me a teasing smile. "After a couple of weeks, you will miss me enough to forgive me. Just remember, it might take me a day or two to get to you if I have to travel partly by conventional means."

He leaned in to kiss me, but I stopped him with a whisper. "Have you?"

"Have I … what?"

"Travelled by plane? Or train for that matter?" We'd taken a few taxis during our trips to London, paying cash. But we mostly just walked.

He laughed quietly. "I might be an arrogant asshole, Dusk, but I'm more than capable of conquering mundane travel. For you."

He waited for a response.

I was probably supposed to gush and be flattered.

I wasn't that easily assuaged, though.

But because it might be months before I got to kiss him again—or kiss anyone, for that matter—I brushed my lips against his, savoring the warmth of his touch and the spice of his magic.

A gentle, sweet goodbye kiss.

I pulled away before it became more.

Zeke let his hand drop with a nod. Disappointed, I thought.

"Write me." He stepped away, crossing toward the windows.

"Read my letter. I included the street address."

"I did. But I'll still wait until you write again." He laughed quietly. "I trust magic to find you, rather than the human postal system."

Zeke pressed his hand against the bookshelves set a few feet in from the far window. Energy shifted under his touch. He looked over at me, smiling. "I'll miss you. Say goodbye to Sisu for me."

He could have done so himself. Except he didn't much like my little brother. That lack of goodwill went both ways.

I reached over, folding the piece of paper with the runes and tucking it into Infinity for safekeeping. "Thank you."

He stepped through the bookshelf as if it were an open doorway, without another word. Zeke didn't like goodbyes.

Sisu screeched from somewhere deeper in the house. He was still having difficulty understanding that he didn't need to bring all his possessions with him. Every time he added something to the cases and boxes piled in the front hall, such as the antique toy trunk that usually resided at the base of his bed, the brownies removed it. They believed that certain items—most items, to be clear—belonged to the house. Not to Sisu or me. Or even to my mother, for that matter.

Ignoring the lingering tingle of magic I could feel on my lips from Zeke's goodbye kiss, I crossed around the desk myself, allowing my brother's obvious distress to force me further out of the melancholy I'd been courting since finalizing the last of the travel plans.

The preliminary paperwork had been sorted out with the help of Tawny Sherwood, a junior associate of my mother's lawyer. She operated out of the London branch of the law offices of Sherwood and Pine, but had travelled to the estate two days before to witness the final signatures by way of an intriguing teleportation spell—one for which I'd had to set an anchor point. Doing so had given me an opportunity to practice, even if not to perfect, a spell from the grimoire given to me by the treasure keeper. Tawny was energetic and exceedingly efficient. So among other things and arrangements, I now had multiple bank accounts, a credit card, and passports for Sisu and me. In our new names.

All Tawny had needed to begin sorting everything out was to make a few phone calls and get a few signatures. Still, she had mentioned that a number of the items she'd added to my to-do list couldn't actually be completed until after I claimed the property—both magically and by physically being on-site.

I pulled one of the brass pins free from the velvet backing of the noticeboard, pinning my second note. Addressed to my mother, the note was so detailed, and therefore so thick, that the flap didn't quite close to seal it properly. As with the letter I'd already given to Zeke, I had briefly outlined my new position and had included the address of the house Jiaotu had bequeathed to me. Both notes had been sealed with my personal wax—brown speckled with 24-carat gold. The same colors I used in my ink.

Both the wax and the ink were imbued with my magic, so that no one but the recipient named on the envelope could open my letters. I'd been able to wield the power of the written word in that particular way since I'd first learned to write anything at all.

Unfortunately, the witch spells from the treasure keeper's grimoire were proving much, much more difficult to master. Sisu had successfully cast a few of the basic spells on first try, though his focus had waned after that.

There were other notes for my mother pinned to the board. One was from Zeke. I instantly recognized his handwriting.

Even with everything else going on—actually especially with everything going on—I desperately wanted to see those letters delivered, and to receive letters in return. I wanted my mother home.

Most dragon archivists could walk through the stacks to and from any library they'd spent a significant amount of time within, as Zeke had just done to and from the Giza archives. Though only after the archivist, and the library itself, amassed enough power and energy. It was a transportation system similar to the guardians' portal system, but more personalized. And not without risks.

A rarer subset of archivists—including the bulk of my maternal line—could also slip through time, though not necessarily by intent. Occasionally, if magic willed it, an archivist could simply be stepping from work to home and find themselves in the wrong library—and in a different century. And, as had happened when my mother went into labor with me, that archivist occasionally had a difficult time getting back to her own present day.

Magic was capricious, yes. But it also occasionally moved archivists where it deemed it necessary for them to be. Though those sorts of so-called divine incidents were only ever really known after the fact.

My mother's house and property had been in her family for generations. The estate was used as an anchor point for many archivists. So it was never a surprise to find a long-lost aunt or a great-grandfather I'd never met eating breakfast in the kitchen on any given morning.

Sisu and I were obliged to travel to Dublin by train and plane, but I had no doubt that my mother would be able to cross through into the magical archives housed at the National Museum of Ireland, whether or not I was the head curator. Just as my Great-Uncle Jamal had done when that archive had been besieged by a soul sucker playing at being a pharaoh. The same creature now presumably imprisoned in its sarcophagus, which the guardian Bixi might well have been keeping as a coffee table.

I still hadn't noted the events of Dublin in Great-Uncle Jamal's biography in Infinity. And perhaps I should link it to the sparse info I'd pieced together about the guardian of Northern Africa—

"Dusk!" Sisu's stressed howl echoed through the corridors and into the library.

I sighed, then turned away from the noticeboard, away from all the books I'd touched and worshiped since first learning to read.

It wasn't only magic that moved archivists where it willed. Occasionally, tasks were doled out from guardian dragons as well. Though I had never heard of an archivist standing before five guardians at once while getting the life she'd thought she'd been building turned upside down and inside out.

Or maybe I hadn't actually been building anything at all. Otherwise, I would have been able to address Zeke and his abrupt demands with more…maturity. Instead of ignoring him, knowing that the passage of time would take care of the answers he wanted. One way or the other.

Sisu was perched on top of the pile of trunks and boxes at the base of the stairs in the front entrance, glowering. The boxes held my books. A meager collection when compared to the library I was leaving behind.

My brother's light-blond hair was sticking up, his clothing rumpled. As if he might have gotten physical with one of the brownies. But knowing that the brownies wouldn't have tolerated any violence, it was more likely that Sisu had been wrestling over the possession of something specific with one of them, rather than wrestling against one of them. Presumably Missy, who actually put up with the young dragon rather than simply pinning him to the ceiling for a few hours when-ever he stepped out of line.

I raised an eyebrow at him.

He rolled his shoulders forward, slouching further into his crouch—his gargoyle pose. "I'm guarding your books," he grumbled.

"The brownies aren't going to take my books," I said mildly. "If I tried to take something out of the main library, a book or an artifact, then the brownies would retrieve it. But these are my books, tied to me and Infin-ity. You know this."

Sisu jutted out his chin sullenly. Then his face crumpled. "Missy won't come with us."

I closed the space between us, smoothing my fingers through his hair. He turned his face away, pretending he didn't want the comfort. I persevered, though, pre-tending I was tidying his white-blond locks. He needed a haircut. I should have thought about that before buying the plane tickets.

Sisu wasn't the only unhappy person in the house. The brownies—Mistress Brightshire, her youngest brother, Job, and her great-niece, Missy—were dis-tressed as well. So much so that I hadn't actually seen any of them since I'd informed Mistress Brightshire of our pending move. Thankfully, the head brownie had agreed to transport our belongings for us without argu-ment. Well, without much argument.

Mistress Brightshire had tried to convince me that I could come and go from the main estate, commuting daily. But the guardians wanted me living among the Adept. So I'd be leaving the comfort of home and the brownies behind. As would Sisu. He had even less of a choice than I had—and I hadn't actually been asked or been able to negotiate the parameters of our relocation at all.

Cradling Infinity in my left hand, I ran my thumb across the deckled edges of the archive's pages and thought about my to-do list. Following that list, checking items off, would get me through this uncertain phase.

"Dusk?" Sisu prompted. "Maybe if you asked?"

My brother and Missy had an extra bond. The youngest of the brownies had only joined the estate after Sisu's birth so my mother could return to curating the archive in Giza.

"You know how it works," I said, straightening his sweater and backpack. I could feel the hilt of the sword jutting out of the pack, though I couldn't see it. I was going to have to ask him—again—to leave it with our bags. He couldn't take it on the plane. "Brownies choose, either a family or a property. But once they bond with either, they stay bonded unless something major occurs. I can't ask Missy to break her bond with the estate for you. I'm not certain it's even possible for her to do so. They aren't our servants—"

"I know!" Sisu cried.

I stepped back, holding out my hand resolutely. "All right, then. Have you got your watch?"

Grumbling, Sisu fished what appeared to be a gold pocket watch on a long, thin gold chain out of his shorts pocket. The watch was actually looped around my brother's waist, through a hole in that pocket. It tracked the date as well as the time, and would change time zones as we crossed them.

Sisu opened the pocket watch's hinged lid. Carefully. To show he understood the responsibility of carrying it. Magic glimmered from the moving parts of the face, dials and arms clicking into place.

This was the artifact that my Great-Uncle Beckett used to help him navigate through time—though its origin was slightly unclear. Either Beckett had bought it off a street vendor in Paris, or he found the main workings in Paris. And then, happening to wander through the stacks at the Musée du Louvre later that day—and stepping into ten years earlier—he'd found an alchemist who had built him a tool to help navigate further accidental missteps.

Unfortunately for Great-Uncle Beckett, the last time he wandered off after breakfast, he'd left the watch in his room. Over twenty years ago.

"It is going to rain!" the watch muttered with a mechanical whirl. "Constantly."

Sisu giggled quietly.

Yes, the timepiece was a little...glitchy. It had a habit of randomly announcing changes in the weather that weren't particularly accurate. As well as pending demon incursions that, more often than not, actually occurred. Announcing out loud. And not always in English.

Which was why it normally didn't leave the house.

But because I really didn't want to miss our flights, I'd liberated the watch from its case in the library and tied it to Sisu the previous morning. Keeping my brother occupied and us on time. Hopefully.

"And have you got our itinerary?" I asked, running through our checklist a final time. "And your passport?"

Sisu tucked the watch back in his pocket, carefully hiding the gold chain as I'd asked him to do. "Memorized," he said, then he patted his pack. "And yes."

"I'm expecting you to keep us on time. We don't want to miss the train or our flight."

My brother sprang off the trunk, landing and grabbing my hand at the same time. "I've got it all mapped out," he said earnestly. "But we won't discover the gate until we check in at the airport."

Tawny Sherwood had explained traveling by plane, and across borders, to us in detail, from our arrival at the airport through to unloading in Dublin. She'd mentioned something about remote or mobile check in, but that sounded too difficult for our first flights. Plus, I hadn't purchased a phone yet, or another tablet.

While most of the Adept had ties to the human world—it was impossible for them to navigate their daily lives without such things—dragons, and archivist dragons specifically, walked through the world unhindered by things like passports and the need to book flights. We used portals, and other doors that I had no ability to call forth, to travel instead.

I really did have to stop running my own memorized list in a loop in my head. Obsessing about it all. I'd already sorted each task by most important to least, then by timing. It was past time to get going.

I cleared my throat, eyeing Sisu's backpack pointedly.

Sisu looked around, pretending he didn't know what I was alluding to.

"The sword," I said gently. "You know Tawny told us that we have to be careful about what we bring on the plane."

He scuffed his boot on the gray granite floor. "But you have Infinity."

"And you have the egg." Allowing him to keep the golden egg in his backpack had been the first of numerous compromises. But we were packed and ready to go, so I was marking it as a win.

Of course, if the egg hatched on the plane, ten plus kilometers in the air somewhere over Sweden or the United Kingdom, I was going to have a lot of explaining to do.

Sisu muttered under his breath, still looking at the floor.

"Louder, please."

"What if I have to protect us?"

"From the humans?"

He scoffed.

"I've packed my daggers," I said, tugging up the sleeve of my sweater to show him my bare arm. I had actually fed the daggers to Infinity. The archive was currently anchored to one of the boxes of books, so I could pull the weapons, if needed, within seconds.

The bone dagger that had once been wielded by a guardian dragon was a different issue altogether. It was currently strapped to my leg under my plaid skirt. Tawny had warned me against carrying it when I'd asked her to check the spells I'd placed on the blade, but Jiaotu had been clear. I was to take it with me everywhere. So I had to hope that the spells I'd struggled to place on it—and which Tawny had verified—would hold.

Sisu reached over his shoulder and grasped the hilt of his currently invisible sword, unsheathing and revealing it at the same time. My brother placed the short steel blade reluctantly on his trunk. Then he patted it sadly.

"It will be waiting for you at our new house," I said. At least if all went as planned.

Behind us, the front doors swept open silently, propelled by magic wielded by brownies who were just as silently mourning our leaving. My throat clogged, but I was careful to not squeeze Sisu's hand too hard. He didn't need to know that I was as anxious as he was.

My brother glanced around. No one came to say goodbye. He bowed his head, breathing shakily. I stared out the door and tried to keep my own breathing even.

Sisu looked up at me, squaring his shoulders. "We need to start walking. We're going to miss the train."

"Okay. You lead the way."

With only our backpacks, we strode toward the open door. I brushed my fingertips against the wooden jamb and whispered, "Thank you," as I passed through.

The door remained open behind us for the entire time it took us to walk the length of the drive. It was still open when we stepped through the gate that marked the boundary of the estate, magically and physically, and crossed into the actual world.

The world in which we were now supposed to live, to make a new life. On our own. With just each other for company, for support.

I squeezed Sisu's hand then, glad to have him with me. He hitched his pack up, ready for the walk to the village and the commuter train station. I really didn't want to know what he was carrying to make it so heavy, and seriously hoped whatever it was didn't get us into trouble at the airport.

Then my little brother laughed to himself. Excited.

Me too.

CHAPTER FIVE

WE PAUSED ON THE COBBLESTONE SIDEWALK AS THE sun set, staring at a wrought-iron gate that appeared to lead into a courtyard nestled between two brick buildings. Our new house number was worked into an intricate design at the top of the gate. The taxi we'd taken from the airport had dropped us off on the corner.

Sisu was trying to look everywhere at once, but I only had eyes for the gate. And the large keyhole set at its very center.

An Indian restaurant stood to our left. Its few outdoor tables were empty in deference to the cool evening, though the interior was packed with customers. Quiet chatter filtered out onto the street. More and more lights from apartments above the shops winked on as we loitered on the sidewalk.

I could feel the weight of the old-fashioned iron key in my pocket. The natural magic of the world filtered in around us as dusk approached. The moment of my birth.

If I was going to start a new life, it seemed like the appropriate time to do so was upon me.

And still, I hesitated. Gathering more information, more knowledge, about my surroundings to be better prepared, I told myself.

Lying to myself.

A bakery was situated on our right. Currently closed. Only three tables in its small seating area. Across the street, up a few buildings, and beside a small grocery store, a dark-windowed bookstore occupied the far corner. The upper storeys of the brick and stone-faced buildings that towered over either side of the street appeared to be apartments. One of which was presumably our new home.

I hoped the Indian restaurant offered takeout, because Sisu was going to need more food within the next hour.

My brother tilted his head, nodding toward the gate. "Magic."

"Yes. I see it."

The twisted iron of the gate was indeed drenched in power. Presumably something to make humans look away, as well as to keep the magically inclined from crossing through. Not that they'd be able to without the key currently in my pocket, of course. The address had also been magically obscured at first glance, the numbers 888 only slowly resolving themselves within the iron whirls and curves as Sisu and I approached. The number eight was considered lucky in China, and since the property had once been owned by a guardian dragon, the street address made perfect sense.

Sisu looked up at me, his hand still cradled in mine. As it had been for almost every moment since we'd left the estate. "Do you think that means other Adepts live around here?"

"Maybe. It would certainly be a waste of space if it was just you and me in one apartment. If the rest of the building was empty."

A light mist kissed my face as I stared up at the darkened, white-painted sash windows overhead. The architecture had shifted as the taxi traversed the city from the airport, centuries all mixed together from Georgian to Victorian to ultramodern. The immediate area and the building we were currently standing before were pure Georgian, though the small gardens that would have once been set before each terraced building had presumably been absorbed when the streets were widened.

Feeling the sun dip below the horizon somewhere beyond the buildings, I stepped forward, pulling the simple iron key out of my jacket pocket. I had borrowed a vintage brown-leather jacket from my mother's closet, pairing it with a dark-gold wool sweater, a brown plaid skirt, and my favorite brown lace-up boots. I still hadn't been able to persuade Sisu to wear pants, so he was in black shorts and a sweater layered under an oversized navy hoodie.

The deed was in my backpack, along with Infinity, but I'd kept the key close to hand for the entire trip. I'd passed through two customs inspections without anyone noticing the bone dagger strapped to my thigh.

I wasn't certain why I'd felt the need to physically hold the key as we travelled from the estate to Dublin, by train, two planes, then taxi. Subconsciously trying to imprint my magic on it, perhaps.

The iron key slid into the lock at the center of the gate without impediment. It was a strange place for a keyhole—so presumably it was the magic that was being unlocked, more so than the gate itself.

I tightened my grip on Sisu's hand.

Then I turned the key.

Energy slipped over my fingers, tickling up my wrist and feathering up my forearm. I felt it seek out and touch the deed tucked into my backpack. Then the gate clicked open.

I glanced at Sisu, withdrawing the key.

My brother grinned, any concern over the location momentarily forgotten. Keeping hold of me, he pressed his other hand to the gate, swinging it open on thick, heavy-duty hinges as he dragged me with him into the courtyard.

We passed through an invisible barrier of energy. That magic momentarily stretched around me, then dissipated. Likely boundary wards.

Then we just stood and stared.

Because it wasn't a courtyard beyond the gate.

There wasn't an entrance to an apartment or a townhouse. Or to anywhere else in the entire building.

No.

What had Jiaotu said …? That the dagger went with the house? A dagger that had belonged to a guardian dragon who'd passed away two centuries ago. And the so-called house had been her…

Palace?

Jiaotu had deeded me a priceless weapon. And a palace.

The cobblestone pathway and the iron gate at our backs were the only parts of Dublin proper that remained. Though the cool autumn air, the light mist, and the sunset still tinting the clouds at the western horizon informed me that we hadn't stepped into a dimensional pocket, as did the lingering sounds of the city. With the building gone, I could now see that horizon without impediment.

But we had definitely crossed into a magically sealed section of Dublin, hidden behind apartment buildings that were themselves centuries old.

The property leading up to the house was at least eight hectares of wild grasses, speckled with sporadic gnarled trees and out-of-control hedges. Edged by what appeared to be a forest that also stretched around the back of the house. Walking slowly, it would probably take ten minutes to reach the main entrance from the gate.

And the house…

The house was…

Taking advantage of my shock, Sisu wiggled his hand from mine, yanking his previously invisible sword from the sheath in his backpack. He nearly caught me in the chin with the tip of the steel weapon.

For gods' sake. The sword should have still been at the family estate, with the brownies waiting to transport it once I'd claimed the new property.

Sisu bellowed. Propelled by a wild burst of magic, the fierce noise rolled across the overgrown lawns to reverberate around the house.

I was going to have to stop calling it a house.

Our family estate was big. Overly large, even. With twelve bedrooms, multiple bathrooms, parlors and sitting rooms, a dining room, a huge kitchen, and the library.

But this was…ridiculous.

The gate clicked shut behind us, taking the lingering noise of the city with it.

Only moments had passed.

Nothing responded to Sisu's declaration of war, though I could feel a subdued energy under my feet. As I would have expected from an estate built by a guardian dragon, then occupied by other dragons for centuries—including Jiaotu's father. Dragons naturally fed the magic that fueled us back into the world.

Sisu took off, holding his sword overhead as if he planned on running all the way to the house and attacking it.

Maybe 'manor' was a better word to use.

Though I was pretty certain that what I was looking at—and what I thought might be English Renaissance architecture—was actually a palace. It was the three towers that really sold it, with the central tower rising taller than the outer two. Or maybe Jiaotu's estate had originally been some sort of country house? Before the city had encroached upon it?

Another item for the to-do list: research the property and figure out what I was supposed to be calling it. It probably had a name, though I didn't recall one from the deed. But naming it would be easier than just repeating 'palace' or 'manor' inanely over and over in my head.

I started up the path, noting other pathways threading through the overgrown grass. Ahead, Sisu suddenly darted off to the right, as if he'd seen something in the misshapen hedges. Their appearance suggested that they had been trimmed into specific shapes at one point. And the fact that they weren't, along with the grass being so out of control, made me wonder how long the property had been in decline before it had been put into stasis.

As in, did it even have electricity?

Or running water?

I lost sight of my brother. A flock of birds went airborne from the hedges, cawing indignantly.

"Sisu!" I called.

"Swallows!" he cried, running toward me, sword hanging at his side.

He was going to—

Sisu tripped on the sword. He went down. Hard. Tumbling across the lawn and losing hold of the weapon.

He ended up on his back, sprawled at the edge of the cobblestone path just ahead of me. A pathway of destruction marked his wake, torn grasses and churned earth. When dragons fell, they fell hard.

"You're lucky you didn't stab yourself," I said mildly, continuing up the gray stone path to the double set of front doors.

Sisu jumped to his feet, brushing himself off. His gaze was as fixated to the house as mine was.

The entrance had been carved out of dark wood. Literally. As if the doors and the doorframe had been shaped from a prehistoric tree that was still rooted in the earth, anchoring the entire house. A heavy brass knocker hung at the center of each door, under the fierce visage of a carved wolf, teeth bared. I tilted my head, and the image of a raptor carved above each wolf resolved itself. The massive wings of both were flared, talons ready to strike.

The design didn't match the door in the nexus, which was all icy grays and whites. This door was more wild, fierce. Brutal. But the similarities were obviously intentional.

I revised my first assessment of the architectural style. The house might have appeared to be inspired by the English Renaissance with its stone facing, its use of glass, and its external strap work, but it had been custom designed. Wolves and raptors were not a common renaissance theme. As far as I knew, anyway. I wasn't well versed in such things. There had never been a reason to educate myself on English architecture, or Irish for that matter.

The keyhole set into the dark-wood door was much smaller than the gate key. But as I stepped forward to unlock the door, the iron key shifted and adjusted size in my hand. It was the master estate key, I presumed, though I didn't expect that Sisu or I would need to unlock either the gate or the house again after crossing through the first time.

"Shouldn't we knock?" Sisu whispered, pressing against my leg.

"It's our house." I gave the heavy door a push. A gray-streaked white marble floor spread out before us. More Italian than English.

No lights. No rugs. No furniture. Not even a table set just inside the door for hats and gloves. Or, in our case, backpacks. An expansive cathedral roof topped the huge central room. I had the impression of stepping into an ornate renovated church, but without the pews, altar, or stained glass. That would definitely explain the central tower.

"What about the brownies?" Sisu whispered. "Shouldn't we have knocked for them? That's polite, right?"

"There are no brownies," I said.

"What?" Sisu gasped. "But... but... dinner!"

"We'll order in takeout." Both terms were unfamiliar to me, but I'd read enough modern literature to understand how it worked, including every magazine I could get my hands on during our trip. Infinity was still sleepy and sluggish, so I had just read them normally instead of feeding them into the archive. "You saw the restaurants we passed on our way here."

"And breakfast?"

"We'll figure it out."

"What about our clothes?!" Sisu wailed. "I'll get all dirty and stay dirty."

I grinned at him, desperately trying to hide my own clamoring doubts. "Remember how Tawny Sherwood mentioned that the electricity and water services might have to be turned on?"

He nodded.

"This is all part of that."

"The to-do list," he said, calming down.

"Yes."

"Okay."

"We could also stay in a hotel for a few—"

"Nope!" Sisu darted into the dimly lit great room, leaving his sword forgotten in the grass.

With no Missy to retrieve it for him.

I stepped back, grabbed the weapon, then crossed into the house myself. As I stepped onto the marble floor, energy contracted around me. I paused, allowing it. Dragons were inherently immune to low levels of magic. But if the house needed to scan me to accept my presence, then I wouldn't block it.

Technically, I owned it all now. Empty palace, wild grass, misshapen hedges, and all.

A two-bedroom apartment sounded like heaven.

And yes, I understood that I was probably in the minority when it came to liking tidy, small spaces. Among the dragons, at least.

A whisper of energy flickered to my right, and our trunks and boxes appeared. Mistress Brightshire had sent them from the family estate.

So my claiming of the property was official. According to magic, at least.

Two large wicker baskets and a tray topped with smaller covered dishes appeared beside my boxes of books. A large Tupperware container holding the cinnamon blueberry rolls I'd baked the previous morning—knowing I was going to need a multitude of bribes to get Sisu through this transition—sat on top.

I smiled at the inclusion of the extra baskets. Mistress Brightshire had sent us dinner. And, I assumed, other food supplies. I just had to hope the refrigerator worked. The cooling spells on the perishables wouldn't last more than a couple of days.

But before I could see what did or didn't function in the house, I had one more thing I needed to do to truly claim the space for myself. An instinctual need that had tugged at me the moment I'd entered, only increasing at the sight of my boxes of books.

Sisu zigzagged past me, moving between a room on the right through to a doorway on the left. I closed the exterior door behind me, losing a chunk of the light.

I set the shortsword on top of Sisu's trunk, then grabbed the top box of books. Carrying it with ease though it was full, and having a destination in mind but no actual idea of where I was going, I wandered into the first large room on the right.

The library was massive, just like everything else in the house. Easily three times the size of my mother's library. The bare hardwood floor gave way to corniced bookshelves of even darker wood, spanning the length of three walls, stretching up to the high ceilings. Two fireplaces were set between shuttered windows on the exterior wall that ran to my left. The library was indeed large enough that—before central heating had been invented—it would have taken two fireplaces to keep it warm.

Heavy gold brocade drapes edged the windows, pooling on the hardwood floor. I didn't take the time to open the shutters to see what part of the grounds the library overlooked. A desk—judging by its shape—covered in multiple dust cloths sat in the far left corner, just offset from a window and backed by more dark-wood shelves. Any wall space that wasn't covered in shelves was wallpapered in royal blue. Darker spots denoted where art had once hung, which made me wonder why the estate had been allowed to degrade before being placed in stasis. A brownie would never have allowed such sun damage to progress so far, especially not in a library.

I paused, giving my eyesight more time to adjust to the minimal lighting.

A library.

A desk.

It was bereft of books or other furniture, but... it was mine.

Mine to fill, to cherish.

Though I had only two boxes of books and a couple of artifacts to start with.

Rapid footfalls thundered overhead as Sisu darted between what I assumed were bedrooms—and hopefully bathrooms—on the second floor. His power trailed him through the house in a stream, coating the walls, the flooring, and the minimal furnishings that he passed. He'd zigzagged through every room off the central great room, but I could feel that he hadn't stepped inside the library.

Sisu was either exploring or having a panic attack. Since he wasn't prone to panicking, and was clearly demonstrating reason by not entering the library even though he'd discovered it ahead of me, I didn't attempt to corral him.

The library was mine to claim.

Even my five-year-old brother knew it.

I crossed into the ever-darkening room, making a diagonal from the doorway in which I'd been hovering. The shutters blocked most of the lingering sunset, but my eyesight was adaptive. I paused near the middle of the longest wall of bookshelves, which were tall enough that a ladder wouldn't have been amiss. I could see a brass track affixed to a wooden runner under the top set of shelves that ran the length of the wall, but no sign of the rolling ladder that presumably once attached to it.

I would have to put the ladder on my ever-growing to-do list for the house and...

No.

Not...just *the* house.

My house.

I set down my box, then turned to scan the dark, empty library. Again.

My house.

My responsibility.

Admittedly, that was slightly overwhelming. Technically, I had another seventy-five years until I reached my majority. Most archivists didn't hold a senior position until then. Or start a family.

Though the job I'd been sent to Dublin to perform, under the guise of mixing into the everyday life of the Adept, wasn't a typical senior posting either—since it was usually held by a witch.

But the house was mine.

So even if the job didn't last or work out, I was...this was my home now. My responsibility, yes. But also just mine. My space. My place.

I touched the shelves nearest me, swearing I could feel the wood grow warmer under my fingers.

Any book I claimed and fed into Infinity would be shelved within this library now. Any artifact or vessel. Anything that needed to be held in my care. Which meant that not only did I need to tie Infinity to what was now my physical personal archive, but I also needed to place wards on the shelves and possibly the library as a whole.

I had no idea how to do that.

At home, I had simply anchored Infinity to the bookshelves my mother emptied for me, what with the family estate already being so massively shielded. The estate being in its own dimensional pocket was actually a side effect of that, though those defenses had more to do with Sisu being the son of a guardian than with Mom being a powerful archivist, from a long line of powerful archivists. Either way, additional wards on my shelves at the estate would have been ridiculous.

While the power to create a personal archive like Infinity was inherent to all archivists, the way our magic was called forth and applied was completely individual-istic. And physical collections—any books or objects claimed by an archivist and then fed into a personal archive like Infinity—were usually smaller subsections of larger family libraries.

The main library at our family estate was large and eclectic, holding documents and books stretching back three generations. Over a thousand years. And one section of it was bonded to my mother. When she col-lected books and magical items specific to her position as head curator in Giza, she filed those within the main collection of the Giza archives, making them accessible to many different Adepts. But whatever she claimed per-sonally appeared on her shelves in the estate library—or, more specifically, on one of the two tables beside her desk, to then be shelved.

Books claimed by another archivist could be ac-cessed only by that archivist, until death. I knew. I had tried to slip through Mom's wards on multiple occa-sions, hoping our blood tie would confuse the boundary magic just enough for me to read what was held on her shelves. It didn't. Just like when I had tried to touch her personal archive, each attempt only resulted in singed fingers.

Some lessons I challenged with regularity. I was always certain that rules were inherently changeable, amenable. Situational.

Other sections of our library had been warded by other family members, whether currently in residence or wandering. Grandparents, great-aunts, and so forth. Zeke's books just piled up around his bed, wherever he was currently sleeping. As my mother's assistant, he hadn't established his own residence. Most younger dragons didn't—even those who fit that label only by circumstance.

Zeke had lost more than three hundred years, not aging, bound up in that copy of *The Iliad*. The cleverly disguised trap had been immediately claimed by the treasure keeper himself. Not shelved by my mother or Zeke. Presumably the book had been destroyed, though most archivists preferred to preserve everything we could. The only reason the book hadn't killed Zeke was because he was a dragon. But as far as I understood, he had fought for his life—over and over—as the tale unfolded, reset, and replayed around him.

I ran my hand over the empty shelf before me. It was dust-free, having been held in the stasis spell that had encased the property, but it wouldn't remain clean. Not without brownies or preservation spells. The books that must have once filled the shelves had obviously been removed before the stasis spell had been set, along with the bulk of the furniture.

Had everything been collected when Jiaotu-who-was handed her mantle over to the Jiaotu I knew, in the early eighteen hundreds? Or perhaps after Jiaotu's father, who'd once been Suanmi's lover, had died? That later timeline seemed to fit slightly better. And, completely selfishly, I hoped it meant that the house had updated wiring and plumbing.

Regardless of everything else, though, the library was now mine to claim. I could tie every single set of bookshelves to myself if I so desired.

The value of this gift was staggering. And now that I was beginning to understand that, I also understood that it came with a staggering number of strings attached. Not even including whatever strings were hidden in the smugness that Suanmi had emanated when Jiaotu agreed to deed the house to me.

Pushing thoughts of things I might never understand out of mind, I sank to my knees, grinning rather than overwhelmed. I pulled Infinity from my backpack, setting my personal archive in my lap. A whisper of languid energy hummed from its worn leather binding.

I opened the cardboard box, grabbing a book at random. *A Concise History of the Modern World.* A new acquisition, though it was used and wasn't terribly modern. I'd read it out loud to Infinity before allowing the archive to absorb it. Doing so strengthened our connection while I absorbed the information myself.

I set the book back down on the other books in the box for a moment, pressing both my hands to Infinity in my lap. I pooled my energy under my palms, twining it around the archive. Infinity was receptive, but not as present as it had been before the coffee shop incident. Keeping one hand anchored on the archive, I grabbed the modern history book and set it on the shelf directly across from me, continuing to hold Infinity's spine.

I smoothed my magic over the book, anchoring it to the shelf and to Infinity. I pressed my power, coaxing it to spread across the bookshelf, claiming the shelf as I would claim a book or an artifact.

Footfalls pounded down the stairs, cut through the great room, and faded as Sisu dashed into another room. A front parlor, I thought. I'd passed through it myself while looking for the library. But with no furniture in any of the rooms, it was hard to be certain of their individual purpose.

A wash of my power simmered before me, coating the book and the shelf, but nothing else happened.

Apparently, warding the bookshelf wasn't going to be as easy as just thinking about it while half distracted.

Silly me.

I released the modern history book, leaving residual magic behind. I hadn't managed to give that energy any sort of intention, so it slowly dissipated. Feeling clumsy and a little ignorant, I hesitated, uncertain if I should shelve anything else until I figured it all out. I was itching to free my books from the boxes, but I wanted to do it correctly.

Perhaps only magical items could be warded. It wasn't as if the history book contained any content I was worried about anyone else having access to.

Sisu skidded to a stop in the doorway, slamming his shoulder into the doorjamb. The frame of the house groaned under his assault. Literally. But the wood didn't crack.

Sisu, grinning madly, pressed his hands against the doorjamb, then practically wrapped himself around it and the wall.

"Did you hear that?" he asked excitedly.

"You? Almost breaking the house? Yes, I caught it."

He leaned back, petting the wall and murmuring, "It's okay. I hear you."

If any other five-year-old had spoken to an inanimate object, it would probably be considered cute. Even inventive. But when the five-year-old child of a guardian did it, it was wise to investigate. Immediately.

Abandoning the box of books, I cradled Infinity in my left hand and crossed toward Sisu. I scanned the library again. But this time, I did so intentionally, with every sense I had access to—including my sense for magic.

Magic most often manifested visually for me, though I could read an artifact more deeply when I applied touch. But it was sometimes a scent or a taste or a sound. Magic liked to hide—and from archivists specifically. Not wanting to be uncovered and risk possibly being locked away from harm. Or from the ability to cause harm.

I felt no one but Sisu in the house. There was nothing magical within the immediate area of the library other than the objects he held—namely the golden egg and his shortsword, which he must have retrieved—plus Infinity, the bone dagger, and the books I'd previously claimed.

"See?" Sisu asked, peeling himself away from the doorjamb. "Can you feel it?"

"A creature in the walls?" I asked, hazarding a guess as I closed the space between us.

He frowned. "No." Then he blinked thoughtfully, and his grin reappeared. "You think there is a creature in the walls? Cool!"

I laughed quietly, brushing his hair from his forehead. I really should have asked Missy to cut it, because I really didn't know how. And I quite honestly wasn't certain how humans took care of such things. Barbershops?

The lump in my throat tightened, or maybe sharpened. I'd been ignoring it since we'd started packing, but apparently not well enough for it to go away. "Did you see that Mistress Brightshire sent us dinner? Let's find the kitchen and eat. Or at least find a table ..."

Sisu grabbed my free hand, gazing up at me earnestly. "Run with me."

"Run?"

He nodded, grinning. "Yes! I'm waking it up! It's been all alone for too long."

That was worrisome.

"The house is…waking up?" The house was a better option than a creature possibly living in the walls.

"Yes!" Sisu tugged me away from the library. And since we were heading in the general direction of the wicker baskets and what I'd assumed was dinner, I allowed it. "I'm feeding the house my magic."

"That will just happen naturally—"

"Now. So the brownies will return."

My heart squelched. With guilt, I thought. There was a reason the brownies had left, and that the property had been placed under a stasis spell when Jiaotu's father had passed, rather than maintaining the estate, empty or not. Either the last of the old familial line had died out, or something had happened to run them off. Brownies didn't leave what was rightfully theirs so easily. The fact that so much furniture had been removed cemented the argument that the estate had been abandoned for some reason.

I wondered if the death of a guardian—or more specifically, the passing of a mantle—was a traumatic enough event that even brownies were swept away by the loss, the grief. Despite Jiaotu's father living in the house afterward, maybe there just hadn't been any reason for the brownies to serve him after losing their guardian.

"We can discuss it after dinner."

Sisu shook his head emphatically, tugging me toward the front door and our baggage. "We start here and do one circuit. You follow me. I've already laid a path."

Even given the size of the house, I guessed that it wouldn't take more than ten minutes to race through it. We were both dragons, after all. However, giving in to Sisu's whims would be overly indulgent and might make him difficult later on. Say, at bedtime. I did have the cinnamon blueberry rolls for backup, though.

"Okay." I tightened my grip on Infinity. "One circuit. Then dinner."

Sisu nodded, shifting his stance, readying to spring forward. "Then we'll set lures for brownies."

"What—?"

He took off, streaking toward the stairs. His power streamed in his wake.

Sighing, I let my own magic loose—my brother would make me do a second and third circuit if he wasn't satisfied with my coverage—and ran after him.

I would worry about his assessment that the house was waking up later. After all, that could mean many different things. And not all of them were cause for immediate alarm.

"I picked us rooms," Sisu declared with his mouth full of roasted potatoes. "I only found two mattresses, though."

"Thank you," I murmured, distracted.

It turned out that the house wasn't completely devoid of furnishings after all, though most of it was covered in dust cloths that I'd left undisturbed. We had discovered the kitchen in the basement, and a room with a long table and benches adjacent to it. It was there that we set up to go through the food Mistress Brightshire had packed for us. We had more than enough for three or four meals, including breakfast. Though I wasn't yet certain how I'd cook the eggs.

The shelves and cupboards were bare in the massive kitchen, but there was a tiny fridge and a large sink. No electricity or running water, though, so we would have to depend on the cooling spells on the wicker baskets. I would have to persuade Sisu to go to the bathroom outside, and to use cold bottled water to brush his teeth and wash his face before bed.

Mistress Brightshire had included a single pillar candle and a pack of matches, along with the plates and utensils we often used for picnics. I was going to have to return all of it.

"Dusk?"

"Yes."

"It's okay, right? Even without brownies, the house is cool ... right?"

I smiled at my brother. He had whipped cream on his chin. I hadn't even noticed him digging into the butterscotch pudding. "Very cool. We'll explore more tomorrow in the daylight, figure more of it out."

He ate the rest of his pudding, then eyed mine. I pushed it toward him, packing up the rest of the food and wondering how I was going to wash the dishes. I opted for tidying everything and putting them in the empty sink. Sisu added his pudding dishes, heaving himself up over the edge of the sink in order to reach.

With Sisu in charge of the candle, we wandered back through the dark house and up a narrow set of stairs that led to the great room and our trunks. The upper door that led to the basement was practically concealed in the wall, and situated behind a pillar. So servants could have come and gone mostly unnoticed, I presumed.

The house was wired for electricity in some fashion, but as we'd searched out the kitchen, flicking the stiff switches we'd passed hadn't achieved any results. So either the property wasn't hooked up to the grid, or it had some sort of generator that needed maintenance. Given that the entrance was off a busy street in the middle of the city, we would presumably pull electricity from the humans' system. Once I figured out how to get that set up. Same with the water.

Thankfully, Mistress Brightshire had sent bed linens and pillows. A third and fourth wicker basket had appeared while we'd been exploring—which made me wonder if the brownie had nipped over to check on us and seen the state of the house. That wasn't her job, but it was kind and helped ease more of my uncertainty.

Despite the heavy drapery and the wooden shutters, the vast rooms of the house had chilled as soon as the sun set.

"Blow out the candle, Sisu," I murmured. "We don't want to accidentally drop it while carrying our trunks."

Sisu obliged without protest. A clear indication that he really was tired.

I grabbed the extra wicker baskets with the linens, and Sisu picked up his smaller trunk. Together, we prowled up the dark stairs. And though our family estate was always filled with light, the dimness wasn't at all unpleasant.

Sisu pushed open a door midway along the main upper hall with his foot, leading me into a room with vibrant green wallpaper, dark wood accents, and a large sleigh bed. The dust cloths that had been covering the bed frame and other furniture had been crumpled and tossed to the side. The mattress most definitely needed to be replaced.

A small bookshelf was built into the wall above a writing desk in the far corner. Sisu had already set his golden egg on the desk, along with his current notebook and pen. He dropped his trunk at the foot of the bed, then took the candle to the desk and relit it.

In contrast to the main floor of the house and its occasional pieces of furniture, more than two-thirds of the upper rooms were empty. In Sisu's claimed bedroom, the wallpaper and wood accents were pristinely preserved. I set the wicker basket I was carrying on the floor, then dug out the set of green linen sheets that were obviously intended for Sisu. The second set was brown. For me.

Sisu grabbed one corner of the bottom sheet, tugging it with him as he scrambled over the mattress. Miraculously, the sheets fit, as did the duvet, once it was given a good shake. Well, it wasn't so much miraculous as Mistress Brightshire looking after us. Even though—by tradition—she couldn't keep this estate while being tied to my mother's property, our family estate. As her family had been for generations.

No. Not 'this estate.'

My estate.

That was still … crazy.

"Okay," Sisu pronounced, surveying the room with his hands on his hips. "I'll help you make your bed, then you can read me a story."

I laughed silently, wordlessly picking up the wicker basket.

Sisu grabbed the candle to lead me to the room he'd chosen for me.

After getting Sisu ready for bed, I watched patiently as he carefully removed the plastic wrapper from two shortbread cookies and set them on a linen cloth, placing the offering in the windowsill. The night was cloudy, but a trickle of moonlight filtered in through the open window.

The napkin had come from Mistress Brightshire's wicker baskets, and I'd been served the cookies on the plane but hadn't eaten them. I'd also helped Sisu open the window a crack 'for the brownies.' The sash had appeared stuck, and I'd been worried about him breaking it.

Brownies didn't need the window opened, or even unlocked, to enter a house in which they were inherently welcome. And random cookies wouldn't attract them either. But I didn't voice any of my thoughts to Sisu as he climbed into bed. If he was feeling even a portion of what I was feeling, then I understood his need to actively participate in building our new life. If imagining that he could awaken the house and woo brownies was helping my brother cope, then I wasn't going to question it.

He would ask questions when he needed what answers I could provide. He also knew how to look things up in...

Oh.

We didn't have a library anymore.

"Dusk?" Sisu whispered, tugging the linen-covered duvet up under his chin.

I hummed thoughtfully, closing the curtains though I knew Sisu would be up at the crack of dawn no matter if he could see the sun or not.

"Mom can find us, right?"

I crossed to him, sitting on the bed. "Yes. I left a message on the noticeboard in the library."

He nodded, furrowing his brow. "And everyone else? Zeke and the other grandparents?"

Whenever an archivist walked through my mother's library—whether using a familial bond or an established anchor to reappear in our present—it usually took some time for us to figure out how we were related. Though my father had been an archivist out of time as well, it was only my mother's relations—no matter how very distantly related—who appeared in her library.

"I gave our address to Zeke," I said. "But anyone else will probably just stay at Mom's house."

"Until they can appear here, right?"

I nodded, though I was fairly certain that it would take years to accumulate enough power in the library for my blood relatives to use it as an anchor point. Another in the list of things that didn't need to be spelled out for my brother quite yet.

"Tell me a tale of a Celtic monster!" Sisu demanded.

"A monster?" I said, feigning confusion. "Well, that depends on perspective, doesn't it?"

Grinning, Sisu threw back the sheets, tumbling out of bed to grab his notebook from the desk. Then he climbed back under the sheets, holding the book in his left hand as I often held Infinity.

A harsh well of emotion clamped onto my chest, and I fought back an unusual wash of tears as I tucked my brother back in, covering my emotional state until I could speak normally again.

I had no idea what I had gotten myself into. But far, far worse, I had dragged my brother away from everything he knew as well.

Sisu blinked at me expectantly, his eyesight barely affected by the low light. I'd need to find more candles if I wanted to tackle some of my to-do list. Or figure out a witch light spell. I was supposed to be a Godfrey witch now, after all.

I leaned over my brother, plastering a playfully spooky expression on my face as I recalled a tale from one of the books I'd had Infinity absorb in the guardian nexus. "Have you heard the tale of the kelpie of the green isle, my little dragon?"

"Tell me!" Sisu squealed, delighted.

I laughed quietly.

Then I told him a story I'd read myself only a few days before, while sipping tea across from one of the nine most powerful beings in the world.

The guardian dragons. Aka the reason why Sisu and I were currently in a palace with no electricity or running water or furniture, far from home and friends.

After tugging on wool sweatpants, knit socks, and the warmest sweater I owned, I carried Infinity down through the house and into the library. I opened the shutters on either side of the desk, allowing moonlight to stream in through the windows, but it still wasn't enough light to read by. I'd left the candle and matches for Sisu on his desk.

I retrieved the grimoire that the treasure keeper had given me, then claimed my favorite ink from the open box of books—I hadn't been able to take it with me on the plane—carrying both items and my back-pack to the sheet-shrouded desk. I tugged the sheet away, exposing a dark hardwood workspace with an old-fashioned phone perched on one corner. Crossing around, I found a matching wooden chair on antique rollers tucked against the desk.

I set Infinity, the grimoire, the bottle of ink, and my backpack on the desk, rifling through the drawers. Two wouldn't open, but I wasn't about to bust into them in the dark. The center drawer yielded a half-melted tapered candle and a brass holder. I took the candle and the grimoire, stepped into a pool of moonlight, and settled down on the cold hardwood floor.

Given the fact that I was actually descended from dragons of lore, it seemed rather pathetic that I couldn't simply whisper a fire into one of the fireplaces. Though from a practical standpoint, not only would I have to gather wood from somewhere outside in the dark, I'd also need to worry about whether the chimney might be blocked.

I opened the grimoire to the page I'd marked when studying it in between bouts of packing. I was posing as a witch. Therefore, it would be exceedingly odd if I couldn't do some basic witch spells. I'd had some success in making flame before, but each attempt had been rather … large. I'd actually singed my hair and eyebrows the first time, sending Sisu into a cackling fit—during which a vase filled with lilies from the garden had also gotten destroyed.

I might have been a little overwhelmed by everything, but I didn't want to burn down the house.

I set the grimoire before my knees, leaning over just enough that I could read the instructions but not block the moonlight. I took hold of the dry, hard wick of the candle.

Witch magic was about intention. Sorcerers focused their power with written spells and artifacts. Shapeshifters honed and built on natural abilities through training and repetition.

And dragons were simply pure energy manifested in a humanoid form. We could conduct and wield that energy. We could hold and contain that energy. Our power grew with age, as it did for most Adepts. And yes, we had to learn to harness it, and some of us manifested different talents. But it was unusual for an archivist to bear and raise a child who wasn't also an archivist. Or, conversely, for a warrior to have children who wanted to wield a pen instead of a sword.

As the child of a guardian, Sisu might take after Jiaotu in power, manifesting skills in glamour or enchantment. And he'd be naturally stronger and faster than other dragons, whether warriors or archivists. I seriously hoped my brother didn't figure out how to turn invisible, though. Not while he was under my care, at least.

The point was, I was magic. Therefore, I could technically wield it. I just needed to not overdo it.

I read the witch spell, step by step, three more times. Then I focused on where I held the candle wick. Murmuring the spell under my breath, I sent a pinpoint of energy—carried on the intent of the witch spell—to my fingertips.

Power sparked, and a tiny golden flame kissed my fingers.

Lovely.

I withdrew my hand, shut the grimoire, and carried it and the now-lit candle back to the desk.

Infinity was still slumbering. So much so that the archive's lethargy was starting to concern me again. If trying to connect the archive to the Internet had actually damaged the magic that bound and fueled it, I didn't know what I would do.

I set the candle next to the archive, making a mental note to watch for dripping wax, as I didn't want to ruin the finish on the desk. Then I unpacked my backpack, placing the pens I'd deemed too precious to box up in the center drawer of the desk. I had a few blank notebooks and other supplies—notecards, drawing pencils I never used, and so forth—in the boxes, but I would unpack them tomorrow.

I took my time with the ritual of filling my favorite white-gold fountain pen with my favorite ink—a deep, rich brown with a dusting of 24-carat gold. The gold in the ink and the pen nib were receptive to my magic.

It was time to tackle at least one thing on my to-do list. I wouldn't be able to sleep otherwise.

I pulled the last items from my backpack, including the leather roll that contained the deed to the property and the thick package of documents from my lawyer. We'd used our passports and the credit card while traveling, but I hadn't dug through all the other information. I'd need to buy a safe for the legal documents. Or figure out if one of the drawers that wouldn't open was already a safe.

The phone rang. Trilling. Loudly.

I blinked at it. Stupidly. But then I was as shocked as I'd ever been. A phone should have needed to be hooked up to a service of some kind.

The phone rang a second time.

It would wake Sisu.

I picked up the receiver, which was set up similarly to the phone in the library of our family estate.

"Um, hello?"

"Hello." A woman. Speaking English but not with a British or American accent. "This is Pearl Godfrey. To whom am I speaking?"

Pearl Godfrey. A witch. *The* witch, actually. The head of the witches Convocation.

"Ms. Godfrey," I said, pleased that none of my confusion was apparent in my voice. "This is Dusk."

"Ah, yes. My long-lost great-niece." She sounded ever-so-slightly amused.

"You've spoken to the Guardian Council, then?"

"No." She laughed quietly. "But I have been spoken to, in a manner. A letter arrived through my grandson-in-law, Warner."

Warner. Jiaotu had mentioned a dragon named Warner who was connected to Jiaotu-who-was. Her lost son. But I'd had no idea that he was also connected to the witches, or to the Godfreys specifically. A dragon, a son of Jiaotu, was married to a witch?

"It must be late there, Dusk," Pearl said, not at all thrown by my silence. "Dublin, yes?"

"Yes, Ms. Godfrey."

"Auntie Pearl," she said. Her tone warming. "If you wish."

"Thank you, yes."

"I won't keep you, Dusk, but I wanted you to know that I've already sent a message to Mesa Byrne, the head of the Byrne coven, to introduce you. As the guardians...requested." Pearl's tone was precise, clipped but not cold. "The coven is mostly centered in and around Dublin, but it has members across the east of Ireland, including Northern Ireland. A separate group of witches oversees the west of the island—the Murphys. Traditionally, the two covens are at odds, but that shouldn't affect you. As a Godfrey."

I could hear the uptick of amusement in the elder witch's tone at that last pronouncement. Given her position, Pearl Godfrey was likely the most powerful witch in existence—without resorting to black or blood magic, I presumed. But apparently, she still found tasks dictated to her by guardian dragons humorous.

And things that delighted powerful people were often detrimental to those lower on that power scale.

Again, I wasn't quite certain what I'd gotten my-self into. Though sitting at the moonlit desk in a mostly empty palace that I'd just claimed as my own, it was some comfort to have a cohort. Even if she was decades older than me and living on another continent.

A rustle of paper came over the otherwise clear connection as Pearl picked up the conversation again. "I imagine you are busy getting settled with your brother … Sisu. Shall I have Mesa pay you a visit tomor-row? She'll likely send one of her children. I have the address."

"Yes." I wasn't going to be able to keep the house or the extent of the property hidden from the witches. If it had even been hidden before I removed the stasis spell. More likely, the Byrne witches had always known that something was magically shielded behind the wrought-iron gate. "Thank you."

"The relationship between the Byrnes and the Godfreys is cordial. And always has been. So you don't have to worry about that. I'm sending you a copy of the Godfrey family tree, and I'll add you and Sisu where I think it's easiest to explain why you just now came into your inheritance. My estranged Great-Aunt Claret never had children—as far as the family knew. So I think it easiest to branch you and Sisu from her, with the inherit-ance triggering on your twenty-fifth birthday. Magic can skip generations."

My mind was whirling with all the possible ways all of this could crumble, would crumble. Deception wasn't my strong suit. What exactly would happen if I was outed as a dragon to the Byrne witches or my employees at the National Museum of Ireland? I was a creature of myth and legend in the flesh.

"Ms. … Auntie Pearl?" I cleared my throat, my mind snagging on something practical, actionable.

"How exactly are we talking right now? Are you … did the guardians give you a phone number? If so, can I have it?"

She laughed quietly. "Are you on a phone?"

"I am. There's one on the desk in the library of the … estate. But the house doesn't appear to have any electricity, so I'm not quite certain how it's working. I mean, I understand that the wiring is different … that it's a different thing than the lights or …"

"Well, I am currently kneeling before an open portal in the basement of my granddaughter's bakery. Jade's bakery. Cake in a Cup. In Vancouver, British Columbia, Canada."

That was impossible. Delightfully so. "A guardian portal?"

"Indeed. I was just about to leave. I have some errands that I needed to do. But I felt the magic tug me away from my afternoon tea."

"The portal … spoke to you?"

"Let's just say it woke. And when no one walked through it, I felt like it would be a good idea to investigate."

"And then you heard my voice."

"Yes. So now we know. Though I doubt the guardians will take the time to connect us again, so once you have everything up and running, perhaps you can text or email me your cellphone number."

A cellphone. I was going to have to get one. Though I didn't know how long it would withstand my magic, even if I was careful. Perhaps the Byrne witches would know a tech witch or sorcerer. "Yes. Thank you."

"I'll courier the information I think you need now. But it's perfectly reasonable for us to not have actually met face-to-face, or to know each other at all, so I'd just stick with that."

Relief washed through me. "This happens, then? Inheritances?"

"Oh, yes. Unfortunately, families do get divided. Sometimes through no fault of their own. And since the Adept live long lives, passing magic and money through their familial lines, often an entire estate can sit in stasis. Surely your lawyer explained the mechanics to you?"

"Yes. I was just wondering how common it was."

"Too common. The Byrne witches won't question it. If you can pass for a witch, that is."

"With my specific skill set, I believe I can."

"You're replacing ... " More paper rustled. "You're replacing Celeste Cameron as the head curator of magical antiquities at the National Museum of Ireland. Ah, yes. Celeste died in that unfortunate incident. Was it five years ago now?"

"Six years. My Great-Uncle Jamal was called in to help deal with the soul sucker. He's mostly recovered."

"Oh. I am sorry."

"Thank you."

"I can't believe it's been six years. Mauve Cameron, Celeste's cousin, turned everyone who applied down, so despite the circumstances, the Convocation will be happy to have the position filled."

"Will ... appointing me cause a problem?"

"No." She laughed quietly, but without humor. "No one says no to a Godfrey." Pearl's tone turned crisp, efficient. "Your magic or how it manifests isn't anyone's business but your own. As a Godfrey, you aren't required to join the Byrne coven. I suggest being polite, of course. But there's no need to prove yourself. Witches have all sorts of talents."

A small fissure of warmth opened in my chest, though Pearl's tone had grown more and more clipped as she spoke. "Sisu might be an issue," I said, almost whispering. "He's only five."

"All young magic users, whether they are witches or shapeshifters or necromancers, manifest magic in odd ways. Often wildly. If I recall correctly, Mesa Byrne's middle child, Ridge, has an affinity for stone. All the Byrne witches practice earth-based magic, and all have absolutely ridiculous names." She sighed somewhat dramatically. "Anyway, Ridge took down the front face of the Byrne country estate just outside Dublin when he was seven. Then he couldn't focus anywhere near that level of power for over ten years. It took them two years to fix what he tore down in a ten-minute tantrum." She laughed quietly, almost as if to herself. "Any idiosyncrasies that Sisu displays will be written off as that." She paused for a moment. "Call or text me anytime." Then she rattled off a number.

I grabbed my pen, flipped open Infinity, and jotted it down. "Thank you, Auntie Pearl."

She laughed quietly again. "Get some sleep, Dusk. The guardians..." She paused, as if correcting herself. "Tasks for the guardians can be...draining. Even overwhelming."

She said it like she knew. Or perhaps as if she'd watched someone else struggle with such a task. Maybe Warner?

"I'm not quite certain what they want of me." I hadn't admitted that out loud to anyone. I really didn't have anyone to talk to. Given time, Zeke might have become more accepting, but until he got used to the change in our relationship dynamic, he'd be testy. "Other than just...to be among the Adept."

"Forging connections. And now you have me. So you've made your first successful foray. And it might just be that. For now, at least. I'll help in any way I can."

"Thank you."

"Goodnight."

The connection between us died before I could say goodbye, but I didn't feel quite as lost and confused as I had before. I set the phone down on its cradle.

Energy shifted to the right of my elbow. But before I could do anything more than spin to face it, a wooden chest appeared, occupying a quarter of the surface of the desk. The energy that had brought the chest to me dissipated. Dragon portal magic, not brownies.

Having grown up in a house full of archivists, I wasn't entirely thrown by items—never mind other dragons—appearing out of nowhere. But the sheer volume of unusual appearances and occurrences over the last couple of weeks was definitely starting to throw me.

It was possible I was overtired.

I had never needed to struggle to be brave as much as I had in the last weeks. Weeks in which my entire life had been picked up, examined, and then swung in another direction by a group of demigods.

At least I had Sisu with me. And though that felt utterly selfish, I knew that tackling this transition alone, leaving him behind, would have been impossible.

I turned the chest toward me. Residual magic tickled my palms—and the chest was damn heavy. But whatever had been literally dropped onto my desk didn't appear to be malicious. I moved the candle closer, then ran my hand over the corner of the desk where the chest had appeared. A brush of magic rose at my touch. I angled my head and squinted.

A burnished circle marked with gold runes was anchored to the desk. Not physically carved into the wood itself, but definitely adhered to it magically, hovering just above the smooth, dark surface. I would have to study the combination of runes and copy them into Infinity to be certain, but apparently, items could be delivered to the house via the guardian portal system.

Following a hunch—even though ignoring whatever the chest contained was already starting to chafe—I lifted the old-fashioned phone from the desk and angled my head again. It was sitting over top of a smaller but similarly rune-marked circle.

So anyone could call me. They just needed access to one of the guardian dragon portals. Interesting. Though mostly useless—unless I could claim either spell for myself, making it work both ways. Or perhaps I could use the runes as my own drop point, like the one in the entrance of the family estate?

The iron pin that was shoved through the hasp on the chest should have been useless as a locking mechanism, except that it had been shoved into place by a guardian dragon. A bit of information I picked up as soon as I touched it. Jiaotu, to be specific.

The pin resisted my pull, tasting my own power before yielding and falling into my hand.

I flipped open the domed lid. Iron and wood creaked.

The chest was filled with treasure.

Literally.

Gold coins and gold bars. Jeweled rings, brooches, necklaces. A small dagger tucked to one side that was most likely only good for spell work or display. A pearl bracelet. A sapphire-and-diamond tiara.

The remainder of my so-called inheritance from Jiaotu, aka the cash and other items he'd promised.

I groaned.

Trust a guardian to not understand that even though he'd just dropped a fortune in my lap, I would now have to sell it. Slowly. Piece by piece. And I had no idea who to even contact to do so.

Pearl Godfrey would know. The elder witch would be happy to act as an intermediary, though I didn't doubt she'd take a fee. A witch didn't hold a seat on the Convocation, let alone head it, without being wily. Tawny, my lawyer, could probably arrange it as well. There had to be numerous options in London.

But as Pearl had just suggested, it would be better to forge relationships on my own, in person. That was the entire point. Though either witch could still send me in the right direction. Dublin was a hub for the Adept. There would be plenty of sorcerers or witches interested in acquiring some of my newfound wealth. And even with the need to deal with gold coins and tiaras, Auntie Pearl's advice to keep everything as close to the truth as possible made complete sense.

Funnily enough, Sisu would have no problem understanding the concept that we suddenly had a new aunt. He'd already met a grandmother and two great-uncles, including Zeke, who'd wandered into his house for breakfast or dinner. Though he'd been quite young when Aunt Josephine had last appeared, popping in on one of the rare occasions she forced herself to leave her archive in Crete.

I shut the lid on the chest, realizing that the candle and the moonlight reflecting off the pile of gold and gems was starting to bother my eyes. And the energy emitted from too much discordant residual magic haphazardly piled together wasn't helping. The pressure eased the moment the lid closed, letting me know that the iron banding on the chest had dampening properties.

Which meant the chest itself might be more valuable than anything it contained. To me, at least. Archivists always stumbled upon items that were ultimately better tucked away. It was part of our power set, just like how the blossoms and the leaves I pressed into Infinity found their way to me. Though that was unique to me. Among my family at least, and as far as my mother knew.

I would examine the chest and catalog its contents in the daylight.

Tomorrow.

Or the next day.

Sighing, I surveyed the items on the desk.

It was silly to try to tackle anything by the light of one candle. And I was feeling off again—hyperaware of the space between me and Sisu, with him asleep all the way upstairs.

I capped my pen, cradled Infinity to my chest, and picked up the candle. I would deal with unpacking and figuring out our housing situation tomorrow. We needed water and power, at a minimum. Because I really, really could have used a hot bath. Sisu had picked the perfect bedroom for me, just down from his own. The adjoining bathroom had a large claw-foot tub big enough for two.

Not that I'd be inviting Zeke into my tub anytime soon. The last time, he'd complained about getting his book wet, completely misunderstanding the point of bathing together. I hadn't bothered clarifying, more than happy to soak on my own.

And that was almost certainly the root problem in our relationship. Neither of us was interested in putting the other above all else. I couldn't imagine raising a child or entwining my life with someone who didn't, when the opportunity presented itself, want to towel dry me, carrying me to the bed still damp. Or who I didn't ultimately prefer to my own company. Or even my baby brother's company.

Maybe those feelings would grow.

But as I climbed into a bed that wasn't quite yet my own, I understood why I had avoided formally inviting Zeke to live with us in Dublin. He could have easily commuted after getting someone to establish the pathway for him. But the thought hadn't even entered my mind. And that was on me, not due to Zeke's inflexibility. Or his hatred of change.

CHAPTER SIX

"WITCHES!" SISU HOWLED GLEEFULLY FROM THE HALL. Then the door to my bedroom crashed open, and a small, heavy body landed across my quilt-swathed legs. "Witches at the gate!"

The mattresses—too soft for my liking—groaned in protest at the abruptly added weight.

Wait ... this wasn't my bedroom.

I cracked open my eyes, matching the bed's groan with one of my own. I'd forgotten, just for a moment, that we were in Dublin. And that I had a new home and a new bedroom. The space around me felt all wrong, lacking energy.

"What?" I managed to say.

Sisu had burrowed under the top layer of blankets, and was now crawling around the foot of a four-poster bed that was twice as large as the one in my room at home. I'd added all the extra quilts I could find in the middle of the night. Apparently, so-called palaces got cold, even for a dragon. Though when I'd checked on him, Sisu had been happily sprawled across his bed, radiating heat like a small star. That was his natural state.

Light streamed in through the windows. It had been so dark the previous night, with the moonlight already gone from the sky by the time I came upstairs, that I'd forgotten to close the shutters and heavy curtains before I scrambled into my cold bed.

"Witches?" Ugh, I really needed to brush my teeth. They felt thick. "Here? What time is it?"

Sisu popped his head and shoulders out of the blankets at the base of the bed, tugging the timepiece out of his pocket and flipping it open. "Three minutes since I last checked!"

Well, that was helpful.

He tumbled to the floor, barely taking the time to make it to his feet before taking off for the hallway.

"Wait for me!" I shouted after him.

"I'm grabbing my sword." He disappeared from sight, then he howled. Literally. The sound echoed through the main corridor, rattling the hinges on the open door.

It was a dragon battle cry, intended to freeze enemies in abject fear before even the first advance on the battlefield. Sisu had picked up the habit the last time Jiaotu had kept him too long. When he'd come back different. Shaken. It was an easy guess that his demigod father had uttered that cry within his son's hearing, but Sisu had never shared the circumstances. Not with me, at least.

I half fell out of the bed, still blinking into the too-bright morning. I hadn't slept well. And that was an understatement. My mind was foggy now, but it had been whirling endlessly as I'd stared into the dark a few hours earlier, feeling the vastness of the empty house around me. The empty palace. After a couple of hours of chilly sleeplessness, I had almost climbed into bed with Sisu. But I needed to at least pretend to be the older, mature sibling, so I'd confined myself to simply checking on him.

Energy shifted up my spine.

The witches Sisu had mentioned were requesting entry at the gate. And probably not for the first time. Unfamiliar with the muted energy that coated the house and was veiling the property from nonmagical sight—as well as finally having fallen into a deep sleep—I'd missed their first 'knock.'

Pulling fresh underwear and a tank top from my trunk, I silently acknowledged the request and informed the outer boundary ward that the witches were welcome. On to the property, at least. They would still have to wait at the front door, of course. But hopefully, I could dress and brush my teeth and hair as quickly as they could walk the front path.

New magic tickled my wide-open senses as the witches stepped through the gate and onto the property. Narrowing my focus, I could actually feel the earth respond to each of their footfalls. Three in total. Byrne witches, as Pearl Godfrey had predicted. The elder witch had mentioned their natural affinity to earth magic.

"Oh. My. God!" The red-haired witch standing directly before me pressed her hand against her chest, inhaling as if she were actually having trouble breathing. Then, with her eyes darting all around my head and shoulders as she tried to get a glimpse of the interior of the house, she gushed a second time. "It's…it's perfectly preserved. I had no idea this property even existed! Even mother was intrigued by the address that Pearl Godfrey forwarded! And look at it! The collection of old-growth trees in the park alone…oak, elm, ash, beech…but then the forest. I'm…I'm…and the house…and this walnut door! It's still rooted into the earth! Deeply!"

She hadn't even glanced at me. Or Sisu. Or introduced herself. She was utterly enthralled by the estate.

To be fair, so was I. Just not quite so gleefully.

"Oh my god," the witch repeated.

Sisu shoved by me, eyeing the newcomers standing before our front door distrustfully. I had persuaded him to leave his sword just inside the door. His bedroom would have been better—farther out of reach—but he'd balked.

The Byrne coven had indeed sent three witches. The youngest appeared to be around my age, while the eldest—the one currently gushing—was no older than her midthirties. None of them looked old enough to be the head of the coven, but Adepts did age slowly. Or they used magic to mask or enhance their appearances. The trio on the front stoop bore enough physical markers in common that they appeared to be siblings—in a way that I knew Sisu and I really didn't.

"Ridge...the house..." the witch continued, flapping her hands as if she couldn't bear to continue. "English Renaissance but with a Northern European influence rather than Italian. The towers! The west wing!"

"Yes," the taller, broad-shouldered male witch at her side said agreeably. "It's gorgeous."

He didn't sound quite so in awe.

"Oh my god," the youngest of the trio finally protested. "Some manners?" She thrust her hand toward me. "Ravine Byrne. Call me Vinnie. I hate it, but everyone does. Youngest of the main branch of the Byrne coven. Metal mage. Which is totally ironic, hey? Given that I'm a Taurus."

Ravine's sleek bob was a uniformly deep brown, likely spelled to achieve that effect. She was tall like her siblings, though they both had what I assumed was natural red hair. Her eyes were a vibrant green-blue, her pale skin dusted with freckles that seemed to appear and then fade depending on how I angled my gaze, indicating she wore a complexion spell. She wore a black skirt under an oversized Aran-knit charcoal sweater with calf-high black boots.

I'd never heard the term 'mage' used to describe an earth witch's affinity to metal. And I had no idea why her astrological sign would make the magic she wielded ironic.

I shook Ravine's hand. She clearly had no issue with touching an unknown magic user. But then, I was supposed to be a Godfrey witch, so not all that unknown.

She wore intricate gold bands on each wrist, covering her lower forearms. The design was Celtic-inspired but clearly modern. Her own work, I assumed, given the 'metal mage' title. Though if the bands held any magic other than her own, I couldn't feel it.

"Dusk Godfrey," I said, releasing her hand. "Great-niece of Pearl Godfrey, chair of the witches Convocation. Archivist."

"A newly discovered niece," Ravine said with a smirk. "Much like this pretty bit of property, I suppose."

I wasn't certain if she was implying something or not, so I ignored the comment. "This is my brother—"

"Telutci," Sisu interrupted. "It means 'bear making dust as it runs.' "

Oh no. My brother only insisted on being called by a different name when he was seriously upset or playing. He must have pulled the name Telutci from one of the children's books the library in the nexus had offered him, given its North American origin.

Ravine blinked. "I thought your name was—"

"You may refer to me as Telu," Sisu said, glowering deeply.

I settled my hand on the back of his neck, and he dug his shoulder into my hip almost painfully, seeking comfort. I should have let him carry the sword. Three new people, on top of packing all his belongings, the long trip, and spending the night in a new house, was too much.

And when your father was a demigod who could change his appearance at will ... well, changing his name was a coping mechanism for Sisu.

Ravine snapped her mouth shut. The other two as-yet-unnamed siblings exchanged a look, smiling slightly.

"My daughter Brooke prefers the name Rook, herself," the eldest said. Her smile lingered even as her attention was pulled back to the house.

"It's nice to meet you both. Dusk and Telu." Ravine's brother grinned widely. He was wearing a tweed suit jacket over a sweater and dark-blue jeans. "I'm Ridge. This is our eldest sister, River."

"You are all named after ... after ... " Sisu faltered, not quite certain how to qualify their unusual names.

"Yes," River said, tearing her gaze from the house. "After features of geography." I thought she might have been counting the windows. Her red hair was streaked with gold that became apparent only when she tilted her head to look at Sisu. She was wearing sleek wool slacks and a silk blouse under a designer trench coat that I recognized from one of the fashion magazines I'd picked up at the Oslo airport. I coveted the plaid lining of the collar. "Our mother, Mesa, is the head of the coven. And our father's name is Glen."

"That's ... weird," Sisu muttered, though he wasn't pressing into my leg any longer. "Witches usually have color names. Or plants. Or flowers."

"That's true," River said. "Though your sister isn't named after a color or a flower."

Sisu clamped his mouth shut so tightly that his lips went white. I had no doubt that he'd been about to shout something about me not being a witch, then remembered he was supposed to be pretending at the behest of his father.

"Shall we invite the Byrnes in and boil some water for tea?" I asked Sisu. I could probably manage a spell to boil the kettle, and had seen a canister of loose-leaf mint tea among the supplies Mistress Brightshire had packed.

Sisu hunched his shoulders for a moment, eyeing the witches. "Just bottled water. The stove doesn't work."

"Oh!" River said, smiling brightly. "We'd be happy to help with that. Actually, Ridge and I own and operate an interior design firm. We'd love to see the entire house and help you get it all... updated. As much as you wish, of course."

"Not even a foot over the bloody threshold," Ravine muttered under her breath.

"All right then," Sisu grumbled. "You can come in if you're here to help, but no touching any of Dusk's books." A large grin swamped his face, and he snapped his teeth at the witches. "You never know which ones bite back."

Ridge stifled a smile. "We are forewarned. Thank you."

Sisu shrugged, then pushed around me to open the door all the way. I stepped back obligingly, and the three Byrne witches crossed into the house.

Our home.

Oh, yes. I liked the sound of that, even if it was daunting.

Sisu grabbed his sword and slung it over his shoulder. "Kitchen is this way." He took off toward the all-but-hidden door leading downstairs.

River appeared to be having a hard time navigating her feet as she spun around, taking in the interior of the huge central room. She grabbed her brother's arm and gushed, "Oh, Ridge! It's a...a church enveloped?"

"I see it."

"We need to get on the Conalls' schedule right away. They'll be the only ones able to pass through the boundary." She looked at me, practically glowing. "Plus Kellan does lovely refurbishing."

Ravine muttered something under her breath. It sounded like, "That's not all Kell is going to want to do in this house."

Ridge threw his younger sister a chastising look, steering his older sister after Sisu. "The Conalls will make time."

Ravine closed the door behind us, then stood shoulder to shoulder with me. She was slightly taller than me in her low-heeled boots. "Don't worry. They'll eventually get around to asking if you actually want their help, and to what extent."

"Okay," I said, feeling oddly comfortable with having my home invaded by unknown witches. It was as if they'd brought a calming energy with them. And maybe they did, given their earth affinities.

Ravine grinned at me. "My sister likes girls. Brother likes boys. I go both ways, but you don't, right?"

I opened my mouth.

Nothing came out.

Ravine waved her hand offishly. "It's good to be upfront about these things. And just because Ridge prefers boys, and happens to be in a relationship, new as it is, will in no way diminish my mother's attempts to get him to impregnate a Godfrey witch."

"I am...forewarned."

"Good." She pushed the sleeves back on her sweater, exposing the Celtic bands. "Now, you said something about tea?" The heavy-knit sleeves promptly fell down around her wrists again.

"Um, yes." I looked at the witch, assessing her. She let me look, smiling slightly. "Hey, Ravine?"

"Yeah?"

"Do you know a reputable local antiquities dealer?"

"You got anything good to sell? Or are you buying?"

"Selling. But you never know."

Ravine threw her head back and laughed. "Oh, we're going to be good friends."

"Are we?"

"Oh, yes." She slung her hand through my arm, practically pulling me in her brother and sister's wake.

The three Byrne witches stayed for hours. We wandered through the house, discussing long-term possibilities for modernizing and preserving. I wanted at least two of the bathrooms renovated right away, as well as the kitchen. But Ridge and River suggested that I convert what appeared to be a large sitting room or breakfast room off the main dining room into a full kitchen, instead of trying to renovate the one downstairs.

And I could see their point. Even if brownies ever returned to claim the estate, they'd hate being stuck in the basement all the time. Though Mistress Brightshire must have slipped into the kitchen sometime during the night to take the dirty dishes I'd left in the nonworking sink, then restock the baskets with clean replacements.

Ridge ordered lunch from his favorite 'authentic' Chinese food place, then started sketching ideas for the new kitchen, while River figured out how to access the house's attics. There were three of those, but one was completely empty. She then started to catalogue what furniture we actually had, noting what was useable and what needed repair so she could "put together a proper budget" for me.

A budget sounded like a great idea.

I was rather a fan of lists.

Ravine feigned being disgusted by her sister's 'nosiness,' but then proceeded to open up a pile of crated artwork we discovered in the central tower. She stripped the nails from the crates with just a touch of magic, conveyed with a twist of her fingers. Then the youngest Byrne exuberantly critiqued each so-called masterpiece she uncovered. Heavy on the sarcasm.

Just to rile up River, I thought.

It worked.

That said, it was pretty clear why the paintings had been forgotten in the attic instead of being taken with the bulk of the other furniture. They weren't fantastic. Lots of horses and hunting. I didn't recognize the style of art, but I wasn't well versed in art in general. And since none of the paintings carried any residual magic, I couldn't read them by touch either.

Ridge and Sisu were waiting at the gate for the arrival of the food so it didn't grow cold waiting for them to dash there from the house. Accepting the order, they confirmed that the nonmagical delivery person couldn't see through the wards that coated the estate. Neither had the witches, in fact—not until I'd allowed them onto the property. As I had the previous night, they assumed they were simply standing at a gated courtyard.

With River talking about purchasing dishwashers and food processors and so forth, I'd been concerned that the estate was spelled to turn away nonmagical people, but that thankfully didn't appear to be the case. So we could get deliveries.

That was going to make my to-do list a lot easier to handle.

Preferring to stay upstairs despite the lack of table and chairs, the five of us sat on the floor in the empty main dining room, soaking up the sun streaming through the windows, passing around entrees, and gesturing wildly with chopsticks as we chatted.

Sisu was quiet, but listening to every word. At some point, the Byrne witches started calling him by his actual name and he didn't correct them.

After lunch, and a couple of phone calls, Ridge actually got the electricity working for the kitchen and the water heater. He found the electrical main, as well as a water shutoff, in a maintenance room hidden off the basement kitchen. Apparently, the estate did pull services from the city. But despite the stasis spell that had just been removed, he was still worried about the wiring and plumbing.

The aforementioned Conalls—who turned out to be shapeshifters as well as building contractors—were contacted via cellphone and scheduled to drop by the next morning to start putting together a quote for the things I wanted done immediately. Ridge assured me that Gitta Conall would find me plumbers and electricians of the magical persuasion so they could cross through the boundary wards. Or, if I preferred, she could manage the entire project.

I knew nothing about renovating a so-called palace, and I had a large chest filled with gold and jewels in the library. So, unless I hated Gitta Conall on sight,

I had a feeling I'd be gladly paying for any and all help she could give me.

But other than accepting the 10 A.M. appointment with the contractor, I didn't have another chance to say no—or yes—to anything. And, caught in the midst of the Byrne witches' excitement, that didn't bother me. At all.

Promising to drop off a preliminary budget in the next couple of days, River had to be physically re-moved from the house by her siblings, even after repeat reminders that she had plans that afternoon with her girlfriend. Actually, Ravine was the one doing most of the hauling, as Ridge was still sketching ideas for the new kitchen on a tablet. Even the youngest Byrne witch was covered in dust from spending most of the day paw-ing through the attics.

Sisu joined me to wave the witches through the gate.

"Do you want to go for a walk?" I asked him when they were gone. "We haven't explored the property yet."

He nodded, subdued. Possibly tired, but sad as well.

"You never know what we might find lurking in the woods," I said, gesturing to our far right where huge trees loomed just beyond the unruly grass.

A grin practically exploded across his face. "I'll get my sword." He spun back into the house, pounding up the stairs to his room.

I followed at a more sedate pace, pulling on runners and a rain jacket. The sky across the estate was misting in between sun breaks, as it was in Dublin proper, when I met Sisu at the door.

The entire property appeared neglected, as if it hadn't been maintained properly for at least a few years before the stasis spell had frozen that final state in time. We headed across the open back fields toward the thickest section of the forest, noting a large greenhouse and a number of empty garden beds at the southwest edge.

Pushing through the thickly treed, mossy woods, we discovered a large pond on the northwest corner of the estate. It was filled with some sort of silver fish and at least three aquatic turtles. Sunlight twinkled across the water, sending beams into its murky depths, even as it barely penetrated the trees that blocked our view of the house.

With the tip of his sword, Sisu poked experimentally at a moss-covered tree that had fallen partly into the water. Its roots had been torn free of the moist earth, dead branches covered in long strands of lichen. Some variety of witch's hair, I thought. "No pixies," he said.

"Not yet." Other than the natural energy that continually radiated from the earth itself, the property felt devoid of magic, channeled by creatures or otherwise.

I was having a hard time hiding my own disappointment at that discovery.

"Let's investigate the greenhouse. And I saw a neglected garden of roses off the library. Lots of different types of sprites love thorny bushes."

Sisu shrugged, then trailed alongside me as we crossed back through the dark woods, intermittently tapping his sword against tree trunks and bushes. He was being gentle, leaving no marks, so I didn't admonish him. Though that wasn't any way to treat a blade. Or a tree.

"You can get better food on the streets of Shanghai than here," he finally said, looking at his feet.

"Different," I said. "Different food."

He shrugged. "I didn't say anything."

"Thank you."

"Can we have fish and chips for dinner? Ravine mentioned that place near here. That wraps the food in newspaper?"

"Yes."

The wood abruptly opened up, revealing a glass structure covered in algae and moss. The gnarled trees were encroaching on what appeared to be the main entrance of the greenhouse. It was larger than it had seemed from the distant field.

The latch was stuck, then proved finicky even after I unstuck it. Sisu shifted impatiently as I tried to open the door without breaking it. Then, with no warning, it clicked and swung wide.

A wash of warm air met us, along with the heady scents of lush greenery, moist soil, and…citrus.

Sisu crowded around my legs as we stepped inside, quickly closing the door behind us so we didn't let in a draft.

Three long, low benches ran the length of the greenhouse—which was much, much larger inside than it appeared to be from the exterior—their wood gray with age and wear. The bench bisecting the center of the space was mostly empty. But on the other two, potted plants of all sizes were grouped by type. The largest were tree-sized, brushing the vaulted glass roof. The plants to our immediate right were speckled with fragrant white flowers and fruit. Citrus fruit, to be exact. Various types of limes, lemons, and oranges, including what appeared to be Japanese and Chinese mandarins.

Sisu's jaw dropped, mimicking my own. He lurched forward, but I caught him by the shoulder.

"This isn't ours," I whispered, still smiling. I couldn't stop smiling. I could practically taste the magic in the air.

My brother blinked at me. "You own the house."

"But we didn't grow the plants. Did we? I'm not sure these have even been in stasis at all."

Sisu's brow furrowed as he tried to figure out what I was saying. Then a wide smile engulfed his face. "You think we have a gnome!"

"I think the estate has a gnome," I corrected.

"So...we ask permission?"

"Yes."

Sisu nodded, then very seriously turned his attention to the orange trees nearest us. Passing me his sword, he stepped up to the low bench and scanned each plant.

I took a moment to breathe deeply, steadily. Feeling as settled as I had in days.

Sisu hovered before what I thought might have been a satsuma tangerine, looking over his shoulder and pointing at a bright orange fruit midway up on the plant.

I nodded.

He scrambled up onto the low bench, slipping between and under the branches of the tangerine and the neighboring lemon tree. He placed his hand on the trunk, then tilted his head, listening.

I also opened my senses to our surroundings, catching the whirl of fans slightly stirring the air. The soil in the pots was a rich, deep brown, speckled with green and white. Fertilizer, I thought. But not anything that could be purchased in a store.

"Can I do it?" Sisu asked. "Even if the house is yours?"

"Yes. We should both ask permission."

Nodding, and obviously caught between trying to be serious and being seriously excited, Sisu placed his other hand under the orange he'd identified as ripe, not quite touching it. "Your oranges look tasty," he said, speaking to the air. "My sister and I would love to try one."

For a moment, nothing happened.

Then energy shifted through the greenhouse, barely brushing against me. Almost like a fleeting thought, but without any words.

The tangerine fell into Sisu's open palm. My brother threw his head back and howled, holding his arm and the fruit aloft victoriously. "A gnome!"

Laughing, I reached within the lush green leaves of the plant, cupping my hand under another ripe tangerine. It dropped into my palm without any prompting.

Sisu clambered down from the bench, grabbed his sword from me, and dashed farther into the greenhouse, holding his orange prize above his head. I followed at a more sedate pace, breathing deeply, joyfully, as citrus plants turned into what I thought might have been avocado, then cacao, and possibly coffee bean. Midway through the greenhouse, I found my brother crouched over an indoor pond filled with lily pads and other plants. Part of an automated watering system, I thought. Or perhaps, if there were fish, a fertilization system as well. All tied together by the gnome's magic.

Sisu was cradling the orange protectively to his chest. He turned to look back at me hopefully. "Frogs?"

"Let's watch," I said, settling on the low rock edging next to my brother and smelling the tangerine.

Sisu mimicked my movements. In tandem, we peeled the tangerines, pulling our oranges in half and then sectioning one half. I held a single section of mine toward Sisu, and he held one of his own across from mine. Orange slices hung suspended in the air, as if they were wineglasses ready to toast.

It was a perfect moment, but my heart was suddenly jammed in my throat, knowing that I needed to give Sisu all his options, even if I was afraid to lose him. "You don't have to stay with me. Now that you see how it will be."

Sisu was silent for a long moment. "What? Why?"

"Jiaotu would take you. Keep you in the nexus with him. You could train with the other apprentices. And the brownies would be good company...if you wanted."

"Do you want me to go?"

"No..." My voice broke. "Never. But I don't want you to be unhappy. I love you. I want you to be...here, but you'll have to pretend to be a witch and go to some sort of school. Or at least work with a tutor..."

"I'd rather go to work with you."

"I know."

Sisu glowered. "I need to stay with you. We'll build up the library, and Mom will find us here together, easier. Right?"

"Possibly. But it takes years, decades, for a library to be powerful enough for our family members to use it as an anchor."

Sisu shrugged. "It's the power of the archivist, not the books or artifacts."

"That's part of it, but—"

"And you are powerful. Otherwise the guardians wouldn't have given you a task."

"They gave me this task because I was the only archivist who was available."

"Nope," Sisu said. "I'm going to eat the orange." He touched his slice against mine. A lick of his energy tickled my fingertips. "I want to be here with you. I never want to be anywhere else."

"Okay." The power evoked by Sisu's declaration sank into my skin. Not any more of a binding than he and I already held—a bond of blood and love. But a promise nonetheless.

He popped the orange slice in his mouth, chewing.

I did the same.

The flavor exploded across my tongue, momentarily completely filling, overwhelming, my senses. I savored it even as it dispersed. Sisu gobbled down three more slices.

"I've never tasted anything this good," I said, speaking into the greenhouse. A touch of energy whispered across the hand that I cradled the rest of the orange in, encouragingly. I laughed quietly and ate another slice.

"I heard Papa and Mom talking in the library," Sisu said, his mouth full. "About you."

"When?"

"Second to last time."

Over two years ago, then. The last time Jiaotu had visited Sisu at the estate, Mom had been gone. "What did they say?"

"Just that thing, about you being powerful."

"Mom always says things like that," I said. "About us being smart and quick learners."

"No." Still chewing the last slice of his own orange, Sisu started eyeing what remained of mine. "Papa. He brought you Infinity, but Mom said it was too early for you to bond with your own archive."

Stunned, I gave him the second half of my tangerine, retaining three slices for myself.

Infinity had come from Jiaotu, not Mom?

Sisu stuffed the entire half of the tangerine in his mouth, talking around it. "They fought. He got mad. Said he'd talk to you himself. Mom grabbed Infinity from him, said he wasn't to tell you anything, and then, like, banished him from the house."

"She ... banished Jiaotu?" That was almost beyond belief. Sisu's father. Mom's lover—or so I'd thought. And the guardian of Northern Europe on top of all that. Mom's estate was anchored to his territory. And even if it hadn't been, archivists didn't banish guardian dragons from anywhere.

"Yep. You had the ceremony two weeks later."

I stared at the remainder of the tangerine in my hand, dumbfounded. As far as I knew, guardian dragons didn't offer fledgling archivists powerful archives. Like they didn't generally offer them positions of service, either. I'd read everything I could on the subject of personal archives, about finding them, setting them up. About how they were tied to the life force of the archivist who'd claimed them and weren't ever, ever passed on. Infinity and all the information it contained, everything I fed into it, would cease to exist when I perished. That was why it was so important to establish an anchor to a physical archive, a library.

"So, see?" Sisu said, wiping the juice from his chin with the back of his hand. "You're powerful. We'll wake up the house, and the library will open its doorways."

"Okay ..." I said, my mind reeling over all the information my five-year-old brother had just dropped on me.

A guardian dragon had proclaimed me powerful. He had fought with my mother, gifting me with a magical artifact so I could bind it to my will, to my magic. He'd then deeded me the estate and the bone blade ... and ...

Oh, yes. I was embroiled in something much, much larger than myself. And that mystery, like any mystery presented by guardian dragons, could take centuries to unravel.

Sisu crouched at the side of the pond, peering at me. "Is it bad? Mom fighting with Jiaotu?"

"No. I'm just surprised." I popped the last three slices of tangerine in my mouth. All at once. My eyes teared up—in a good way—as the taste exploded through my senses again.

Sisu poked at the surface of the water with the tip of his sword. The water rippled toward the weapon—somewhat aggressively, I thought. He quickly withdrew the sword, grimacing at me with wide eyes. "It didn't like that."

"No," I said. "It didn't." Then I laughed, and despite the disconnected information whirling around in my head, I still felt content, settled. Magically blessed by the presence of a gnome on the estate. And the helpful Byrne witches, for that matter. I held my hand out to my brother. "So... are you ready for our next adventure?"

He grabbed my hand, hauling me to my feet with a grunt. "Yes!"

As Sisu napped in a large chair he'd hauled down from the attic, I sat down with Infinity at my desk, in my library. Opening the thick book to the first perpetually blank page. I glided the tip of my favorite fountain pen across that page in a swirl of golden-tinted, magically imbued brown ink:

The personal reflections of Dusk Zhi Godfrey
Oct 21, 2021

A deep hum of power emanated from the archive. The paper swallowed the ink greedily. And then new words appeared in the center of the page, unbidden by me or my magic.

Tell me everything.

I blinked.

That was new.

I laughed quietly, completely thrilled, amazed.

Infinity had...evolved?

Awoken.

And, still grinning, as I pressed the tip of my pen to the page again to tell Infinity everything, I realized that the property hadn't been the only thing stuck in stasis.

So had I.

Babysitting Sisu. Training and learning, yes. But mostly just waiting to reach my majority and to be given an established position. A position that would have come with a firmly established set of duties and obligations. And of expectations. I would have been tasked as every archivist had been before me—to diligently preserve the past.

But now I was Dusk Zhi Godfrey, Archivist of the Modern World for the guardian dragons. A title and position created solely for me. No dictated parameters or rules, other than establishing ties within the world of the Adept.

I was going to have to make it up as I went along. To react in the moment. The only rules would be the ones I chose to impose. It was a completely overwhelming but ultimately intriguing prospect that had me pen in hand, scribbling away in my fully awoken archive, and grinning from ear to ear.

ACKNOWLEDGEMENTS

With thanks to:

MY STORY & LINE EDITOR

Scott Fitzgerald Gray

MY PROOFREADER

Pauline Nolet

MY BETA READERS

Anteia Consorto, Terry Daigle, and Gael Fleming.

FOR THEIR CONTINUAL ENCOURAGEMENT, FEEDBACK & GENERAL ADVICE

SFWA
The Office
The Retreat

ABOUT THE AUTHOR

MEGHAN CIANA DOIDGE IS AN AWARD-WINNING WRITER based out of Salt Spring Island, British Columbia, Canada. She has a penchant for bloody love stories, superheroes, and the supernatural. She also has a thing for chocolate, potatoes, and cashmere.

For recipes, giveaways, news, and glimpses of upcoming stories, please connect with Meghan on her:

New Release Mailing List: http://eepurl.com/AfFzz
Personal blog, www.madebymeghan.ca
Twitter, @mcdoidge
Facebook, Meghan Ciana Doidge
Email, info@madebymeghan.ca

Please also consider leaving an honest review at your point of sale outlet.

ALSO BY MEGHAN CIANA DOIDGE

NOVELS

After the Virus
Spirit Binder
Time Walker
Cupcakes, Trinkets, and Other Deadly Magic (Dowser 1)
Trinkets, Treasures, and Other Bloody Magic (Dowser 2)
Treasures, Demons, and Other Black Magic (Dowser 3)
I See Me (Oracle 1)
Shadows, Maps, and Other Ancient Magic (Dowser 4)
Maps, Artifacts, and Other Arcane Magic (Dowser 5)
I See You (Oracle 2)
Artifacts, Dragons, and Other Lethal Magic (Dowser 6)
I See Us (Oracle 3)
Catching Echoes (Reconstructionist 1)
Tangled Echoes (Reconstructionist 2)
Unleashing Echoes (Reconstructionist 3)
Champagne, Misfits, and Other Shady Magic (Dowser 7)
Misfits, Gemstones, and Other Shattered Magic (Dowser 8)
Gemstones, Elves, and Other Insidious Magic (Dowser 9)
Demons and DNA (Amplifier 1)
Bonds and Broken Dreams (Amplifier 2)
Mystics and Mental Blocks (Amplifier 3)
Idols and Enemies (Amplifier 4)
Misplaced Souls (Misfits 1)
Awakening Infinity (Archivist 0)

NOVELLAS/SHORTS

Love Lies Bleeding
The Graveyard Kiss (Reconstructionist 0.5)
Dawn Bytes (Reconstructionist 1.5)
An Uncut Key (Reconstructionist 2.5)
Graveyards, Visions, and Other Things that Byte (Dowser 8.5)
The Amplifier Protocol (Amplifier 0)
Close to Home (Amplifier 0.5)
The Music Box (Amplifier 4.5)

DOWSER SERIES • BOOK 1

CUPCAKES, TRINKETS,
and other
DEADLY MAGIC

MEGHAN CIANA DOIDGE

DOWSER SERIES • BOOK 2

TRINKETS, TREASURES,
and other
BLOODY MAGIC

MEGHAN CIANA DOIDGE

DOWSER SERIES • BOOK 3

TREASURES, DEMONS,
and other
BLACK MAGIC

MEGHAN CIANA DOIDGE

ORACLE SERIES • BOOK 1

I SEE ME

MEGHAN CIANA DOIDGE

ORACLE SERIES • BOOK 2

I SEE YOU

MEGHAN CIANA DOIDGE

ORACLE SERIES • BOOK 3

I SEE US

MEGHAN CIANA DOIDGE

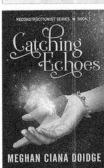

RECONSTRUCTIONIST SERIES • BOOK 1

Catching Echoes

MEGHAN CIANA DOIDGE

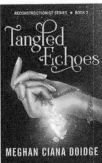

RECONSTRUCTIONIST SERIES • BOOK 2

Tangled Echoes

MEGHAN CIANA DOIDGE

RECONSTRUCTIONIST SERIES • BOOK 3

Unleashing Echoes

MEGHAN CIANA DOIDGE

THE AMPLIFIER SERIES • BOOK 0

THE AMPLIFIER PROTOCOL

MEGHAN CIANA DOIDGE

THE AMPLIFIER SERIES • BOOK 1

DEMONS & DNA

MEGHAN CIANA DOIDGE

THE AMPLIFIER SERIES • BOOK 2

BONDS & BROKEN DREAMS

MEGHAN CIANA DOIDGE

Made in the USA
Las Vegas, NV
14 December 2024

14209654R10125